PRACTICE

PRACTICE

Rosalind Brown

Farrar, Straus and Giroux
New York

Farrar, Straus and Giroux
120 Broadway, New York 10271

Grateful acknowledgment is made for permission to reprint
excerpts from the following material:
Introduction to *Shakespeare's Sonnets*, by Katherine Duncan-Jones.
Copyright © 1997 Katherine Duncan-Jones and
The Arden Shakespeare, an imprint of Bloomsbury Publishing Plc.
Selected Poems, by Rumi, translated by Coleman Barks with
John Moyne, A. J. Arberry, and Reynold Nicholson (Penguin Books, 2004).
Reprinted with permission of Maypop Books.
Between Men: English Literature and Male Homosocial Desire, by Eve Kosofsky
Sedgwick. Copyright © 1985, 2016 Columbia University Press.
Reprinted with permission of Columbia University Press.
"Shakespeare's Sonnets: Reading for Difference," by Helen Vendler,
Bulletin of the American Academy of Arts and Sciences 47, no. 6, March 1994.
Copyright © 1994 The American Academy of Arts and Sciences.

Library of Congress Cataloging-in-Publication Data
Names: Brown, Rosalind, 1987– author.
Title: Practice / Rosalind Brown.
Description: First American edition. | New York : Farrar, Straus and
Giroux, 2024.
Identifiers: LCCN 2023051866 | ISBN 9780374613013 (hardcover)
Subjects: LCGFT: Novels.
Classification: LCC PR6102.R6926 P73 2024 | DDC 823/.92—dc23/
eng/20231113
LC record available at https://lccn.loc.gov/2023051866

Our books may be purchased in bulk for promotional, educational,
or business use. Please contact your local bookseller or the Macmillan
Corporate and Premium Sales Department at 1-800-221-7945, extension
5442, or by email at MacmillanSpecialMarkets@macmillan.com.

www.fsgbooks.com
Follow us on social media at @fsgbooks

1   3   5   7   9   10   8   6   4   2

For my parents

Nuns fret not at their convent's narrow room;
And hermits are contented with their cells;
And students with their pensive citadels;
Maids at the wheel, the weaver at his loom,
Sit blithe and happy; bees that soar for bloom,
High as the highest Peak of Furness-fells,
Will murmur by the hour in foxglove bells:
In truth the prison, into which we doom
Ourselves, no prison is: and hence for me,
In sundry moods, 'twas pastime to be bound
Within the Sonnet's scanty plot of ground;
Pleased if some Souls (for such there needs must be)
Who have felt the weight of too much liberty,
Should find brief solace there, as I have found.

WILLIAM WORDSWORTH

OXFORD

2009

The alarm goes off.

A small spider, sitting in a corner of the dark room, would see her stir in bed, and her hand slow and uncomplaining reach over to the clock. The alarm stops.

She makes a low noise in her throat. Feels carefully for the lamp switch and clicks it. Everything in the room gives a jolt, being lit: as if she didn't do this six mornings a week, exactly like this.

She sits up in bed, takes hold of her glass, and swallows a few mouthfuls of stale water.

Six o'clock in the morning, Sunday, at the worn-out end of January.

Taking a deep breath she lowers her feet out of the bed and gets up: stands for a second. Then goes into the bathroom. She sits there, feeling her pelvis drain itself. Out again with a rush of water.

She twists the window catch, pushes the window open, and puts her head out into the dark frozen morning. It smells cold. A small secret, to open the window before first light. Like the beginning, or maybe the end, of a novel: somewhere, high up in the college, a light came on and the curtains were drawn aside and a window was opened. No one was awake to see a plaited head lean out and breathe deeply, looking down into the dark garden. No one saw her give one last shiver like a flourish and pull the window shut.

She collects her water glass and takes it over to her desk. Switches on the second lamp, which settles the room: to be lit from two angles, this is a system of lighting.

On the shelf is a stack of books. She takes the top one, a small red book, Shakespeare's Sonnets, and lays it in the middle of the desk. Then goes to put the kettle on.

She puts a mint teabag into the waiting mug, then stands there in the building roar of the kettle until the switch pops up in triumph. Lifts the kettle and carefully lowers the spout over the mug. Her bare feet tingle slightly, imagining being splashed and scalded. The teabag is lifted up in the hot water and begins to move, finding its buoyancy, releasing its flavour.

For now she ignores the radiator. She wants the room cold and dim and full of quiet. Eventually she will open the valve, when the cold has soaked through all the layers she starts to pull over her body, sweatshirt and cardigan and thick socks and fleecy slippers, as well as her bright blue blanket, which will take up various relationships with her body throughout the morning: strategically round her waist and thighs, then bunched hanging over the back of the chair when she goes to make breakfast, then wrapped tight around her whole body after she's eaten a bowl of muesli in cold milk.

Right: a calm look at the desk, the room. Has she forgotten anything.

Actually what she wants is to open the window again, she wants to know exactly how the *cold blue light* feels when it begins to appear, she doesn't want to miss a single detail of the *slow dawn*, the *reluctant winter morning*—

'Stop it Annabel' she says softly, out loud. In her world-voice she reminds herself: these phrases don't come from anywhere, they take no responsibility for anything. In a couple of hours there will be daylight and bells clanging languid and far away, and eventually there will be doors opening and shutting in the corridor and people embarking on their own Sundays, and she can just be very quiet here, working steadily into the morning.

She shakes out the blanket, wraps it around her middle, and sits down. Takes her marker out of the book: Sonnet 49. Against that time (if ever that time come). Against that time do I insconce me here. That time being, for her, to-morrow afternoon when the essay is due. Soon she will have to make conversions, into propositional knowledge. But for now she will read, and continue to read, without hurry, searching herself for a theme. When an idea begins to inflate itself she will become purposeful, but until then she will just read.

This is the silence of no phone and no computer, which are both switched off and kept well away from her desk so they don't frizz her thinking so early in the morning. Next to them on her shelves are a row of essential and non-essential books, her files of notes, coffee-making equipment, a small teapot and some loose-leaf tea. She would say the things she does, she does properly. Dried camomile buds in an airtight jar. No posters on the wall, just a couple of small prints they sell to tourists in Italy. Also a small cactus with a precise pattern of white needles over green flesh, in a pot she brought from home.

For basic sense you can read each of Shakespeare's Sonnets in a minute or two. For a little more chewiness and analysis, five or six minutes. The trouble is keeping them apart. Each one seems to annul the previous one: no longer that, but this. They dissolve into a mass of little qualifications and turns and particularities and withholdings and accusations and escapes. To make some speciall instant speciall blest. Let this sad interim like the ocean be. Nor dare I chide the world without end houre. Like the small wheels of a great mechanism, always clicking into new relationships. *Intricate* is the word. *Exhausting* is also the word. The little packed blocks of text. He wrote them over many years, probably, and here she is trying to rustle up a theory in two days and hook it convincingly on.

She takes a sip of the hot clear brownish water: tasting grimly of good health.

Last year their tutor Sara, a medievalist, advised them to spend as many hours as they could simply sitting with the text. Don't keep your pen in your hand, just pick it up when you really need, or else your pen will get ahead of your thoughts. Look away from the text and out the window if you have to, try and pause your mind on the one thing. Focus on the experience of *you* reading this text *now*. But always remind yourself, it *was* written, some time, by someone.

Afterwards when they mentioned this to one of the grad students he said Oh yeah well she's a phenomenologist at best. *At best* she thought was interesting: she wrote the whole phrase down on a Post-it and stuck it on the wall above her desk.

Anyway so she is spending time with these poems: which are better company than people, they take your shape willingly, but still lightly, like a duvet does. She lets them work on her mind, entering wholeheartedly into the spirit of them, hardly writing anything down: just reading.

On another Post-it is written Find the edges and breathe into them, but that was from a yoga teacher.

She turns another page and reads. Time doth transfix the flourish set on youth, And delves the parallels in beauty's brow.

Sonnet after sonnet after sonnet of iambic pentameter: which has raged like a virus through the English canon so it begins to feel like the original metre, the *only* metre, the sole mode of reasonable speaking. How it shifts its weight slightly to accommodate things. Her eyes go to the notes: to transfix meant to pierce, parallels could be military trenches.

This *man*. She tries to picture him at some sort of table, cogitating. His sharpened pen. Or did he stroll whistling through Southwark letting each poem evolve in his head. All day long striding across the stage, making cheerful business decisions, laughing with a hand on a fellow actor's shoulder, a slurp of ale, you're right I'll take another run at that scene, et cetera. Behind all this, the obsession beginning to build in his chest, shredding him from the inside. Then home. Muttering onto the page. The ornament of beauty is suspect. Why is my verse so barren of new pride. It is my love that keeps mine eie awake. It is so grounded inward in my heart.

Four hundred years later, she keeps on reading.

Her mouth comes up against the flabby weight of the teabag. Tipping the mug back and forth she gets it out the way and slurps the rest of the tea from around it. Then gets up to put the kettle on again.

This is how she starts, with only peppermint and water, laying down a nice layerful of liquid for her stomach to start work on. Later there will be seeds, nuts, muesli, banana, milk. Then the glory of coffee: which dictates other things. She has tried yoghurt but it reacted badly with the coffee and produced stomach cramps. Buttery toast with coffee is an especial pleasure but also sometimes produces stomach cramps. And in Bridget's room a couple of weeks ago they dared to put butter and jam on croissants and drank strong coffee, and this produced such agonising stomach cramps she had to come back and spend two hours in her room sipping nettle tea. Coffee is undoubtedly the problem: but also, so dazzlingly, the solution.

Lunch is the strongest part of her regimen, consisting of chopped raw vegetables mixed with pulses and herbs. Supper she still eats in hall. Then goes straight upstairs to empty her bowels. This is regular: seemingly something they put in the food: never planned, but always necessary.

Such small rules as she has, no apples after meals, no coffee on an empty stomach, are surely just the beginning. Soon it will be pork she has to relinquish, being too fatty. Wine, being too heavy and sweet. Giving up one thing exposes her to the next thing, which soon becomes intolerable: like, the more sensitive she becomes, the more sensitive she becomes.

She stands in front of the dark window until the kettle has finished. Then pours more water over the same teabag. As if there might be something in it she missed the first time around. Since her family is well off she must be thorough and heedful in all things, never prodigal. Also she enjoys riding the spectrum from what is officially peppermint tea through something more like flavoured, tinged water. To travel in a lonely country most people wouldn't call *tea*.

Sitting down with her mug (and ignoring her bladder which is beginning to make itself known) she holds her mind firm and reads four sonnets in a row, slowly and with full awareness.

Ah, something, something comes. For a moment there she had him, his sonnet-voice: slick – bitter – nimble: *that* voice. A tiny effortful shuffle forward. It is already gone.

On her lamplit paper she writes down the three words, but for god's sake, the essay is due tomorrow. She needs more than adjectives. She picks a piece of feather off her cardigan and it finds a natural spiral movement down to the floor.

Your friend Will: I've been working on a sonnet sequence, would you read it for me?

How on trend you are, Will. I'm not sure I've got time, Will. Oh, I'll give them a glance if you really want me to, Will. Then sitting after supper with the manuscript in one hand and a cup of wine in the other. By the time your wife says good night you are struggling to control your breathing. Good God. Your friend Will.

She flicks her fingernail against the edge of the desk. Not exactly edifying, a balding man with middle-age spread and an embarrassing infatuation he can't get rid of. At what point does the quality of the work start to redeem the pitifulness of the scenario. At what point does it no longer redeem. Better to embrace silence than to spout the same old shit. Spending again what is already spent.

She turns to look at the window. The beginning of cold light outside, there are dark shapes now against the dark sky. A robin declares something sweet and firm: it expects at any moment to be declared master of the morning. If she turned her lamps off she could really see it, the dawn being put together with great care, or perhaps reluctantly, the morning seeping in, the poem on the page slowly emerging. What if her old teachers could see her now. Pretentious would they think, this fixation on silence and light levels. There is a perfectly reasonable nine-to-five day to be worked in the library if only she, et cetera. But this conviction of it all being one realm: the Sonnets, and the room in which the Sonnets are read.

Anyway she peers and makes out the trees starting to arrange themselves in the distance. Trees, presumably, would laugh at the very idea of a sonnet. But perhaps not: perhaps they have broader responsibilities than she thinks.

It is so still and gradual, this way of getting light. This is why there is the phrase *painfully slow*, because that is how it feels. Hard to convince herself that even this dark blue light is from the sun: with a capital S: the blazing tremendous Sun.

At least winter itself is not painful. Deep winter, no struggle just huddling and waiting, can be of some comfort to her. The arrival of spring *hurts*: those newly invented whites greens yellows against the dark wet soil, everything seems to strain and push: then summer bulges and tips over, begins to sag and parch: and at last comes autumn, relaxing gratefully into decay, into sodden silent winter.

Then again there are already snowdrops in college, and the first green pricks of crocuses, and the days are creeping longer again. Things are already further ahead: the year is turning as it always does.

Her heel is in her crotch. Now the urge to empty her bladder is becoming a *bite*: it nips at the urethra, that most sensitive of flesh-clusters, part of the complex which includes the clitoris. She holds that in her head for a moment, the word *complex*, castles and palaces and priories, little folds and pinches of flesh: like a series of side chapels around the great arched nave of her cunt. Concentrating the sacred forces. Providing a focus for worshippers.

A tiny snort at her own imagery. Back to the Sonnets.

What is it now, just past seven. She focuses on the page. Still feeling a kind of blankness from these poems, they gaze whitely back at her. If only Jonathan would set them essay questions. She has, say, eight or nine hours' work left on this, to pump herself up with reading, to identify a theme and elaborate it and select her key sonnets, to balance them with brief and judiciously selected moments from others, and to find a conclusion that at least appears to peer forward into the implications of what she has said.

But the Sonnets fucking elaborate themselves. They hold no secrets, they are pristine, like bone china. Or they are transparent as water, yes, as vodka: without realising it you're looking *through* them rather than into. Or like ghosts: you come out the other side of them and your sword hasn't had the slightest effect.

After a moment's hesitation she writes this down. Transparent. Vodka. Ghost. At the very last gate of time pressure she may need to return to it.

At last conceding to bodily function she gets up: or rather, emerges from her bundle and heaps the blanket half across the chair half onto the floor. Staggers sideways a step, to her own annoyance. Yoga has made her both more supple and more fussy, with the high standards of a careful practitioner. There are now unsatisfactory ways of walking through to the bathroom.

Bare-bottomed she sits. The urine starts chaotically, it catches on some small vulva-fold and trickles its warmth around, she pushes until her anatomy releases and it becomes a comfortable stream. A long one, like a long exhale. At the end, understands her pelvis all light and clean. She gets up and sees the pale colour of the urine: perfectly usual at this time: she has put a great thaw down through her river-system, of water and peppermint tea, a torrent carrying along all her splintered boughs of trees and chunks of ice. Soon, soon, the dark flame of coffee.

Coming back to her work she leans over the book, palms flat on the desk. Come on. Where is something. She lifts the book, flips to a random page, finds: This is my home of love, if I have ranged, Like him that travels I return again, Just to the time, not with the time exchanged—

Perhaps breakfast.

Actually, as she collects together a bowl and spoon and the box of muesli, there might be an essay to be written on the particular dynamics of the male-male love affair in this period. Both men widely travelling, both freely sociable, and of course their fucking has nothing to do with the question of marriage, no energy is wasted on pedantic negotiations of that sort. The muesli splatters into the bowl and she puts the box down and heads for the door – and there are such men everywhere swaggering about the streets and taverns, as she pulls her door open and puts it on the latch and 'Baaargh' she murmurs squishing her eyes against the strip lighting. But then is there a way for them to be serious about each other – how could one ever demonstrate commitment, as she grabs her milk out of the fridge – how to reach a place of safety and confidence that yes, this is it, we belong to each other – and she pushes back into her room and quietly shuts the door. No. It's more like, there must always be an *until*: it will last, until it doesn't.

Yesterday in Katherine Duncan-Jones's introduction she found this:

> Perhaps there is something particularly attractive to women readers about the enclosed space of 'the sonnet's narrow room', and its predominantly reflective, introspective subject-matter. Possibly, also, women readers are able to remain at once calmly observant of, yet emotionally receptive to, the masculine homoerotic thrust of 1–126 that has caused such upset to generations of male readers.

She copied out the whole of this passage, not intending it for anything, just a comforting dry little joke. A small smile gleaming through the scholarly prose.

Now she crunches and flattens and swallows, staring into space. Would she call herself calmly observant of it. Emotionally receptive, yes – but more than that – there is a sense in which she feels – what is the word – somehow *implicated*. She looks down at the empty bowl, presses a wet oat and brings it to her mouth. Yes they are men and she is a woman: but she is somehow *in* there, *with* them, desperate for it.

Anyway. Now coffee. She stands at the window again with the kettle building to a new boil. Down there over the wall is the garden of the college next door, very neatly kept, the lawn white with frost, the flowerbeds black. Sometimes, on weekdays, two men come and walk around that lawn. One with his hands clasped behind his back musing, about a passage of Aristotle she imagines, or Aquinas or Milton or Matthew Arnold. The other, younger, apparently trying to follow his thoughts. But they laugh too, they examine the odd shrub, then after ten minutes or so circling the flowerbeds they go away. Once they took turns pouring small amounts from a thermos into a cup and drinking from it. She only ever sees them together: never on their own, never with anyone else.

What if she stood naked for them at her window: hair down on her shoulders, breasts a little tight with cold, but her face calm, perfectly at her ease. One man murmurs to the other Don't be too obvious but if you look up there you'll see something rather enjoyable. They would have no way of knowing if she was touching herself unseen below the window. Soon they would be glancing up to her every time. And perhaps one day they would beckon her down, and take her quietly back to a room deep in that ancient college, where finally, finally, she might learn something.

The kettle switch flicks up again. She lifts it and fills the empty cafetière with plain hot water and steam goes up everywhere. Really she prefers an espresso pot on the stove, she likes the thought of water pushed up under the pressure of its own steam, the coffee forced hot and hard through metal tubes. At home there is a whole Sunday ceremony, her feet flatten on the kitchen flagstones while Mum lines up four mugs on the counter, the coffee is black, it has a hot dark smell, the newspaper is dismantled into its supplements and spread out on the kitchen table, Sophy's long limbs are jutting out everywhere, and Caro is curled up in her chair, very quiet and sleepy like a cat.

But she has no stove here, and anyway this is perfectly sufficient, perfectly luxurious. She lifts the cafetière full of hot water, takes it into the bathroom, and very carefully pours it down the sink. This highly breakable vessel. Her previous cafetière she knocked against the kitchen tap and took a beautiful long piece of glass out of the side. Spent twenty minutes wiping all the smaller bits out of the sink with kitchen roll. She kept the long piece for a while, until her scout Maggie pointed at it while hoovering the floor and shouted did she want that disposed of safely, and reluctantly she said yes, wishing a silent goodbye to its long jagged shardness. They sellotaped it up in a piece of cardboard and she wondered what minor research project she had intended it for, that would never be embarked on.

The coffee tips like compost into the wet warm glass. She fills it up with hot water again and fits the top piece in: the completed unit. Takes it and the small brown mug back to her desk, and sits down.

∾

The coffee enters her like a hot dark phrase. Something in its ferocity is deeply excellent: it reaches her stomach and she sighs. She takes another mouthful. *Fuck* coffee is wonderful. It takes hold of things in her mind and starts to pull them steadily apart: showing through like silvery light is nuance, subtlety, intricacy. She *loves* the Sonnets, oh god, their plainness and glitteringness, they sparkle in her head like leaves in sunlight. Be where you list, your charter is so strong, That you yourself may privilege your time To what you will, to you it doth belong. As the caffeine turns things faster all these words seem to pant in her: a word like *privilege* spreads itself out until she is top-heavy, saturated: she could let her head thump forward onto the desk with the weight of it. Every thread is stirred by coffee, like a field of fine grass.

She turns a chunk of pages to another sonnet and breaks into a smile. From you have I been absent in the spring. And this is Sunday morning, no one rushing off to lectures, everyone just getting up slowly and going to play sport or sit in church or eat huge brunches. Her mind always deeply knows what day it is, and no matter how much work she does, Sunday is always somehow a day of rest.

Meanwhile coffee tastes of four hundred years squeezed together now bursting apart. She flips the pages again. The poet is Beated and chopped with tanned antiquity. She notices the insistent glamour: a shabby glamour to be sure, but definitely a sardonic cleverness: she looks round at the bright window, then back to the poem: yes right *here* is the tired and bitter flavour of the old, brilliant, unrequited poet-lover. A cold English winter, men with red noses along the docks at Southwark, why don't you ask Will

Shakespeare, he's been fairly pumping out sonnets lately, the flash of a smile. If you know what I'm saying.

She touches the thought again, to see it moving: the Sonnets as a strange glamorisation of the unattractive poet. Whatever glamour might mysteriously be – and how it might also be shabby – and how that (even more mysteriously) might be the best kind. He *knows* things. What he knows is admittedly fairly fucking abject: but by god is he an expert in it.

Another sonnet. She fixes her attention onto more metaphors about the passage of time and the threat of a rival: the catastrophic development that another poet should dare to write in praise of the same young man. But when your countenance filled up his line. *Oppressive* is another word for these poems. Like two dry hands on a withered heart squeezing, squeezing. The chill of all that white space. Each sonnet requires an ice pick and a hot thermos.

Actually the cold is beginning to take a more certain grip. The usual places feeling it first: the backs of her hands, the whole of her pinky fingers, the upper slopes of her feet. Inside her nose is a slight fussiness, not quite a blockage. She will wait until she is pulling the blanket tighter and tighter to no avail, and then she will concede defeat and go and turn on the radiator. Somewhere in college are the great boilers, running constantly, flooding heat into her room any time she wants it. The problem being that with all the noise and rough heat she never does want it, her eyes will itch, her brain will desiccate.

She takes a breath in, then inhales even further, stretching the muscle fibres across her chest and belly. Holds it with effort for a few seconds, then releases it slowly and feels all the tissues come back to meet. Outside a bird catches the sunlight quickly and is gone.

Ten minutes later she gives in. Levers herself upright all wrapped in her blanket and shuffles across the room: bends down: twists the radiator valve open: and the sound of air rushes in which she knows is really hot water, sealed in a long dark winding space. She lays a hand along the top of the radiator and the heat starts to come faintly as if from a long way off. Now the room is loud. Now convection currents will push dry air past her face. She shuffles unhappily back to her desk and sits down.

How to proceed. *What to say*.

No: she brings her palms together and her nose down to them: gathering back the points of herself, breathing within her own confines. This rage is a fleshly one only, nothing is really the matter. She will find, if not a courageous bold way into the Sonnets, then a stealthy back way in. She will warm up.

By lunchtime she will be getting too blurry for work. Having expended her mind's energies for five or six hours she will address herself to the body: yoga, then meditation, then a long walk. To twist the dial marked Body and the dial marked Mind in opposite directions until they find each other again. Then an early dinner, a bit of pottering in her room, a shower, and so to bed. Certain variations are built in: tutorials on Mondays and Thursdays which she has no choice but to accommodate, Sundays when she often goes to evensong, and Saturdays, her day off, when she buys food and goes to see Bridget and does her washing. And every day she has to catch and deal with little wisps of resistance: but broadly, there it is, the routine is well established, it gathers and directs all her various strengths and susceptibilities.

After a good yoga sequence she can stand in mountain pose with her eyes shut and hands held open at her thighs, and feel the stretches like pools of shimmer in her muscles. Like working and polishing leather, or brushing her hair with a good soft bristle brush. She hates telling people she does yoga, and saying the word *yoga*. It doesn't sound like what it is.

Meditation for the first ten or fifteen minutes is filled with her brain trying to plan, think, hold on. But eventually it gives up and slumps or sits in its own little corner and leaves a luminous space, like a still lake at sunrise. For a while she tried to interrogate this feeling, what are you, where have you come from, and it would blink and vanish. Now she has learned to try and watch without holding on to it, though the fear of it disappearing is constantly in the background. Sometimes comes a random burst of love for parts of her body: her feet, their thick-skinned soles and neat toes, or the delicacy and strength of her hands, or something stranger like her teeth. Then she finds the meditation space as a place of strangeness, nothing really happening, but it morphs and shades itself, and brightens again, in its own mysterious geometry. Also sometimes an instantaneous *sense*, of a film, a person, a memory, which she'd never be able to describe. Her brain can trick her into thinking something is pictorial until the moment she opens her mouth to talk about it: like trying to explain a dream: it's simply mental texture and doesn't come willingly to words. She finds this reassuring, that her beautiful brain can escape language for small moments, even when awake. There is after all something else, that language is *about*.

Walking, at this time of year, means going through the dusk into the dark. Her thoughts become a steady low current, and Oxford moves past her presenting all its people and streets: which she absorbs silently.

Evensong is more in the vein of her repeatedly asking a question, and wondering if she will ever get an answer she likes.

For a moment she surveys her long series of hot meals and movements and solid nights in bed that are directed towards this: the close understanding of poems on a page. It seems both appalling and entirely appropriate. Then she shakes off the thought, and takes another mouthful of coffee.

Some things still need refinement. Behind her the room heaves with possessions, far too many. Every term she and Mum carry crates of her life out of the car through the quad and up the stairs: and stuff this room with toiletries, crockery, sheets and duvets, knickers and cardigans and shoes, her laptop, her files of paper. She brings her own woven tablecloth for the coffee table. Her own coathangers. Her own umbrella.

A mage in Earthsea owns what, three books of lore, some plates and cups, some goats, a small house. When he travels he just takes his staff and his cloak. The main thing that travels is himself. And she thinks of a Greenland shark deep under the ice, sliding with barely a whisper through the blue darkness. The only possession it has is its own slow energy, and this keeps it alive for hundreds of years. While Shakespeare was bounding across the stage and then home to scratch the words she now reads on the page in front of her, that same shark was searching, sensing, growing.

Really, being very strict, the only thing she both needs and wants – both *needs* and *wants*, she repeats to herself – is this, the small brown mug with the tiny cross stamped into it. She puts out a hand and touches its mottled brown glaze, circles its small diameter with her thumb and finger. Its handle is low down on its body, it has a strange shape, a foreign shape. It comforts and ignites her, as if she were an Italian monk. It could accompany her to another existence: she could wrap it in a jumper, put it into a rucksack with a few other bits, and go off to Greece or Persia or Morocco, without Rich, just her alone. Walk straight out of the airport with no luggage and get on a bumpy bus. A dusty knot of hair which will stay atop her head all day. She will be brown and a little thinner, she will move easily through the streets. She will sit in a small courtyard and eat a spare but delicious meal of olives, hummus, extremely good salty bread. Not read, just gaze. Think. Understand subtle, fragile things. Be like the courtyard, holding it all in suspension. Pour water from a glass bottle into the small brown mug and sip, a few molecules at a time seeping into her like a blessing. Take one book only, a wondrous inexhaustible one, the Bible or Homer or Dante, something long and narrative and complicated. When she comes back she will be different.

Actually coming back from Italy last summer she *was* different, in a way she vowed never to forget but did somewhat forget because she never got it properly into pinpointed, representative images. She holds her mind there now. It was something like: her hand laid on a warm stone balustrade at the top of steps, looking down to where all the gravel paths converged, the square of small dark shrubs around a statue. Her mind blinded by heat, only able to see angles and colours, sun and shadow. She did stand there, she remembers, trying to insert real people into the scene. Rich, but he was too vivid, too fidgety, he kept coming over and saying confidential things or slipping his arm around her. Miles she had more success with, he could walk languidly with his thumb stuck in a book and his face lost in thought. Then she was struck by Mum: who as she wandered along the path below seemed to lift slightly out of her own Englishness, a tall cropped-hair figure in a dark linen dress, her eyes like deep cuts: she was not automatically a tourist, she had a native kind of warmth. Which however vanished the instant she came over and started arranging the three girls into a photo with the view of Florence in the background.

Then they came home, and it was late summer in England and there were steady cool winds high in the treetops, dark cool shadows and the delicious tip of autumn beginning to nose in. She read more Woolf novels, made more notes, and gaped at the freshness and beauty of everything. The woods and fields and little rivers. She was still at the beginning, she realised: she is still in love with the Shire after all.

Rumi says:

> Be concentrated and leonine
> in the hunt for what is your true nourishment.
> Don't be distracted by blandishment-noises,
> of any sort.

Of course Rumi was never an undergraduate at Oxford. Whereas. She did well in her first-year exams and was duly heaped with blandishments: a scholarship, a scholar's gown with ruffles to sweep and flounce with, and a scholars' dinner at which there were speeches of congratulation, and so much dark alcohol, and Jonathan and Sara the English Fellows being jolly and patronal. During the speech they slumped against the wood panelling while she sat upright and still. Then afterwards she went down to the bar with Miles and Ciara and they all took off their scholars' gowns and laid them across their laps. She bought a vodka tonic with ice and sipped it very cold. Ciara teased her again for being largely silent and sober. It is amazing how long people will go on being surprised by the same things even after they already know them.

Perhaps the only reasonable part of the whole thing had been months earlier, during the exams themselves, again and again asking her brain for the right word, the right quotation, and it came willingly to her: and she thought, this is an improvement. And after each exam she spent a few minutes sitting quietly in her room and decided that, on the whole, it had gone well.

On the other hand Rumi would probably cancel all exams and simply give each student a mirror. If you recognised your own disgrace and freshened your soul with tears, you would pass.

~

Where was she. Yes, the brown mug. Italy: the sonnet's birthplace, of course: the repetitive, trancelike rhymes of Petrarch, the sighing, courtly *sprezzatura*. Then those fine young Englishmen, Surrey Wyatt Sidney Drayton Shakespeare, got hold of the sonnet by the collar and roughed it up a bit. No more *sprezzatura*: instead a sort of grey, bossy bitterness. More beer! the poet shouts, scribbling a brilliant line about pricks.

She flips to another sonnet at random. You are my all the world, and I must strive To know my shames and praises from your tongue. Mark how with my neglect I do dispense. Yes it's there: a sort of baldness in the tone, plaintive, and domineering. Also splintering, and exhilarating. She writes some more words in her list – rough, bossy, bitter, plaintive. How he insists again and again on his own enslavement while remaining absolutely in charge.

One day perhaps she will be someone about whom people say, she's read everything. They'll ask her if she has read a particular text and she will simply reply Yes, with no drama, just an understated massive erudition, like suddenly the ocean floor opens up and the sheer vastness of her reading and knowledge comes into view, dark blue and receding into further darkness.

From one angle her determination to work rather than drink or fuck glints like the single-mindedness that one day becomes greatness. From another angle it looks wrong, but even kingfishers don't always catch the light in the right way.

Her body is starting to crawl with irritation: her nails are too long, her lips are dry, her mind is going all fuzzy and homogenous, with no power to separate or refine things. Sometimes a deep itchiness in her ears, or in her cunt, or right in her bones. Across her scalp little nerve cells jerk one way or the other for no reason. Loose hairs suddenly visible on the desk or looping out wide from her cardigan catching the light. Tiny painful flaps of skin starting to peel around her fingernails. An almost constant need to take water in and push water out: sometimes she can't wait to get off the toilet and flush so she can neck some more water. Where the thinking is supposed to happen, how anyone can think in these conditions, is a mystery.

Case in point: there is more hair out of her plait now than in it. It gathers round her ears and leaks pieces down her neck. She could brush it all through and redo the plait excellently tight. But all the long hairs falling flickering down to the floor. Instead she reaches up behind her head, holds there the pleasing tug through her shoulders, gathers all the puffy slept-on hair and arranges it into a knot she can drag the hairband over. Takes her hands away: it stays. Good. Now it will leave her alone.

The hiss of the radiator, and its hot air. She makes a noise of annoyance. Up and over she goes with a kind of sonnet-lunge, and turns it off. Mark how I banish heat from this my room.

Then she looks outside. Holy shit. However long it is since she last looked: suddenly there is a huge mist, obscuring everything, gardens, buildings, meadow, all flooded with strange muted white light. As if while she wasn't looking they put it together in the long grass, smiling and holding their fingers to their lips, then said *Now* and it all lifted up in one go. The top of it steamy and cold, disappearing and glinting in the air.

She sits down at her desk again and keeps very still, eyes closed, listing things. Grass. Water. Cold air. Sunlight. She risks another glance out. Near the window is a silver outline down the edge of the birch tree. The mist beyond it is enormous and pale white.

'Fuck' she says out loud: sits for one more clenching moment: then up out of the chair hauling off her jumpers and pyjamas, steps naked to her chest of drawers and pulls out a load of clothes and drags them onto her body. Then coat – scarf – gloves – boots. Grabs her cold keys from their shelf.

Pauses to squint at this extraordinarily quick decision that she really should not be making. Sees her glass of water on the desk, lifts it up and takes one long drink. Then out.

In the porters' lodge she meets big tall Emma Weeting coming back from her run. They say an extremely neutral hello.

All right, as she picks up speed through the first gate and along the lane, half an hour might be good, it's not even nine yet, a walk might invigorate her. This feeling of really *moving*. Because yes, this is one thing the Sonnets do not do. Out here real strides can be made. She cracks a smile at her own non-metaphor. Rich would enjoy that, her being literal by accident, he would laugh in the easy way he has. His eyes would crinkle: with lust never far away.

She ducks through the second gate, and arrives at the huge white expanse she knows to be the meadow. Into it she walks, her face set cold with purpose.

There is the wide bright mist, and then all the lurking objects that come into view as she walks, and then each of her soft footsteps sounding on the packed earth. It is beautifully cold, slightly less beautifully damp. The breaths she expunges are thick and white. Little birds go very fast in and out of the undergrowth, a flicker more in the mind than in the eyes. If she looks up she can see, in places, the top of the mist where it gives suddenly onto the blue sky. Everything is purified. Even white scraps of litter look very clean there in the grass, and all the trees are exquisite with texture. This is a changed world. She is Edmund just arrived in Narnia, astonished and ready to apologise for anything.

But there are other people, of course there are, she couldn't have been the one warm puffing body in all this white mist. A skinny girl approaches, running all lopsided into her joints, she can almost feel the weight of her flinging from one leg to another. She lowers her eyes as the girl goes past and the footsteps fade off: tries to nail her attention again onto the silence.

She takes the avenue of trees towards the river. Behind her the colleges retreat into a single line of buildings, letting her go. She passes a tree: silence: now another tree: silence: now another tree.

Maybe while she is out here she should decide about Rich coming, so the time will not be entirely wasted. After all it was inevitable he would ask to visit her, she should've had an answer ready, it is unconscionable that she still hasn't told him yes or no. He wants to come and relive their first tiny adventure — what, nearly two years ago? — when things went so gorgeously askew. The little restaurant on Walton Street, the Moroccan lamb he suggested she try. The wine. You know I genuinely meant it as a favour to your mum, he insists. He and Mum stood talking after the concert with their violin cases over their shoulders, and she and Sophy and Caro were all clustered round ready to go home, and he said Actually I'll be in Oxford in a few weeks, I'll take Annabel out for a decent meal if you like, college food is so awful et cetera et cetera. He meant it as a favour: he intended to report back.

Her whole front is already wet in the mist, in this chilly decorous morning. A curl of damp hair is stuck to her cheek. Yes it makes a tawdry enough tale: he ordered the red wine which they split, unequally: and there was a moment (unperceived by her) when his mind began to purr and soften. He started to steal food off her plate: and there was a moment (unperceived by him) when she thought, is this really — might I really — I seriously could. He paid and offered to walk her home. Each of them now mentally redacting the report they would make to Mum. They stepped out into the raw February night and he said Fuck it's cold, and immediately apologised for swearing.

They walked. He stopped to point out some quirk of architecture, his hand was on her shoulder as he got her to look in the right direction: and he turned and his head was very close: and there was a kiss. She stood in his dark arms trembling and kissing. He drew her against his body, he asked in a hot breath would it be completely disgraceful if he invited her back to his hotel room. She managed to say, she hadn't – she'd never – and he understood. They walked back to college and he kissed her very softly on the cheek.

But now she had his email address. For two weeks they corresponded, and for another two they spoke almost daily on the phone. Then she went home for Easter: she drove out to his village: in his bed it happened: a sharp exhaustive fullness inside her, and blood. He assured her the sheets would come clean in the wash.

She reaches the river. A certain grey calm starts to settle in, an exhilarated calm. The walk is in her now, she lets her shoulders fall back with every exhale and slows her steps along the bank. A dark shape on the water suddenly shrugs and lifts its neck and becomes a goose.

She exhales hard and it puffs out in a cloud of vapour. Then came the bad period. That email: I really can't honourably justify, you're only nineteen, the secrecy is damaging to us both, your mum trusted me to, you deserve someone who will blah blah blah. Wishing you all the best with your studies. Rich. And silence after that. A few weeks later Mum reported meeting his new girlfriend Carmen and not liking her: which was alternately comforting and enraging.

So she found, firstly, Joseph Waller doing materials science at St John's, who all three times insisted on going to her room instead of his for reasons not obvious to her until she saw him coming out of his own college holding hands with a girl with lots of hair and big sunglasses.

Next things narrowed in on Miles, elusive and pale-mannered Miles, who kept her beautifully, delicately heartsore.

And third in a rush of mercy came Virginia Woolf: who more than adequately filled the months. She read all the novels over the summer and came back to Oxford for her final year seized and clamped with Woolf, she ate less, she worked more, there were new hummings in her brain, her bowels turned ticklish, she lost weight, her sleep began to flicker and bubble, she was cold in the night. She read the big Woolf biography in great gasping chunks, she stormed up Woodstock Road every week for her tutorials, she brought question after question to Patricia: how did she do it, how did she find space in her day and brain and metabolism, in spite of her illnesses, to write and read and talk like that?

Finally Patricia said to her, gently, She was atypical.

She didn't miss the gentleness, and sat there silently wishing the end of term would not come.

Then Patricia said Anyone who studies an extraordinary person has to come up against the fact of not being as good as her, believe me I've felt that too.

That was their final tutorial, and Patricia issued no invitation to come again for tea, or even to keep in touch. As she walked back towards college the afternoon sank into a very cold dusk. She suspended herself in a cafe with a buttered teacake, wrote up a few more notes, then went back to her room and sat in her chair and read all evening, ate a single banana for dinner, and went to bed thinking wildly of a narrow standing desk, and walks on the downs, and a pen endlessly writing, writing, writing. For the next week she typed her Woolf essay in near total silence, that low-stomach nausea keeping her company.

Anyway at last it was judged, by someone or other, that she had waited long enough. She went home at the end of last term and sank straight into the flavour of Christmas, all dark and velvety and erotic. Everything seemed to point to the secret triumph of being pressed against a wall and slowly kissed. And then bumping into Rich in the department store: both of them alone: so brilliant a coincidence she had to double-check she hadn't designed it herself. He hadn't seen her for nearly two years and she knew her lower, quieter voice must be astonishing to him. She watched him employ all his brainpower to keep the conversation going. Was Oxford fun, was she working very hard. Where was Sophy applying to university. Would they all come to the Christmas concert. Had her mum mentioned how difficult the violin parts were, or was she finding it easy, ha ha. Around them the desperate shopping bustle continued, no one was really paying attention to anyone else. It was the perfect moment if he could recognise it. Finally he swallowed his embarrassment among the glassware and invited her for a coffee.

On impulse she pitches this moment at the Sonnets, and something begins to unwrap itself: Will! calls a familiar voice, and Will barely has time to arrange his face, the beautiful boy is there in front of him, teeth white in the gloom, smiling. Let's to the Rose and Crown, we'll toast the coming of Christ together. Will nods. Tight-faced, wild-hearted, he follows his tormentor into the roar of the tavern.

In the cafe Rich said things like Are you seeing anyone, and You know I still think about you a lot, and You talk even less than you used to. She gave a small smile and said, I know. Rich the reliable barometer, he likes to let her

44

know how she is coming across to him, it seems a perpetual fascination. Then they went to a pub and drank mulled wine, sitting close enough at the table that when they wanted their knees to touch it was easy. He put his hand on her thigh and slid it upward and she froze with what he took to be discomfort but wasn't. Perhaps her face had not accurately reflected what she was feeling. A look of lust would have been better: an intensity in the eyes and a faint smile or sneer to convey its full portion of encouragement. So often her lack of smiling renders her unintelligible in the world: and additionally Rich is always expecting her to hesitate. He apologised and took his hand away from her leg and she had to catch it and put it back before he understood.

So now, at nearly twenty-one, she is enough of an official person that Rich apparently *can* honourably justify all the things he didn't quite say in that email: kissing her, fucking her, asking to visit her, plus all the accessory activities that could only be described as *lascivious*: fondling and kissing her neck for many minutes at a time, grasping her flank and squeezing, lowering his face and licking in a long motion the slit of her cunt. Seemingly he has redirected his honour, into unabashed concupiscence: *Annabel* he moans, kneading her.

A sudden noise behind: and then a tall runner in shorts overtakes her, his reddish rough hair bouncing behind him. She sees very clearly the lines of muscle sharpen in his calves and thighs as his feet hit the ground. Morning lust is nicely damp.

The river is totally silent, stretching off into the mist towards the east, towards London. A pollarded willow has put out a spray of thin orange branches. Oh Rich. Perhaps he *should* come and visit. Come to see her in this habitat, like an Annabel-tourist. They can be out and about in chilly Oxford together, then together in a hotel bed under a thick patterned counterpane. Though, actually, all this stuff in the Sonnets, the nervous older lover and the impatient beloved, she is starting to know a little about that. Rich is also Dr Richard French, thirty-six years old, general practitioner, he did electives in emergency wards and watched people die on operating tables, he prescribes opiates every day and briskly comforts old ladies, and once in his kitchen he took his stethoscope and slid the cold disc under her bra so she gasped, and he smiled – but he's afraid of her, ain't that the truth, he fucks her holding his breath. He asks to come and visit, and agonises that she will say no. Everything is tinged now, with his same slight dread.

A different thought: what might she be able to discover about the Sonnets without them gazing coldly up at her. Tries to isolate a single sonnet in her head: she gets monuments and ships, a vial of rosewater, a sulky horse, a pair of dark eyes. Cankers in roses, rotting lilies, a locked wardrobe full of jewels. The foyzon of the yeare which means the autumn harvest. Death's scythe, the black lines of poetry, the Young Man forever green. A phrase comes – *the desperation of metaphor*—

Also the love triangle. The Young Man has slept with, *is* sleeping with, has fully stolen away, the poet's mistress. His and hers infidelities: but the Young Man's is worse. Take all my loves, my love, yea take them all. Subtext: yea take them all, thou greedy selfish shit: a perfect pentameter. And there is also a *pleasedness* there, no? He is pleased to say, Loving offenders, thus I will excuse ye. So dry, so wounded, so haughty, enforcing his own nonsense-logic. For my sake, he repeats: I can perceive, as neither of you does, that this all refers back to me, you're just agitating the waters as I suck them irresistibly towards my plughole. Fuck each other if you like. I, structurally, am the winner.

She completes her lap of the meadow. She has experienced the mist now, her head is coated with damp, and here is the path back to college. Every reason to go back and carry on working.

Her pace slows, and she looks round, at the glitter of sun on wet winter grasses. She has already pulled apart somewhat the tight weave of her routine. It frays now of its own accord: the decision is made: she is going round again.

With legs rejoicing she walks on, a bell sounding in the cold wide air.

Perhaps it's inevitable, but it feels sudden. Something moves in her mind and the SCHOLAR appears, as if stepping out from behind a tree. Tall, solemn, in his black cloak. With pleasure she feels her body take on his taller, leaner body. She is walking the path now with his long careful strides, she is looking up into the trees and over the meadow, studying the mist with his precise eye. Now things are full of pattern and substance and wet luminosity. He understands the conditions that have formed this mist, he notes them and tips the knowledge like a little powder into his mind.

So here he is: walking. He came out intending to solve something complicated about his work. He observes the swollen lumpiness of a plane tree, all the bare branches wet and dripping. But inevitably he is thinking about his friend: if *friend* is even the correct word: the SEDUCER. Not that *seducer* is the correct word either, since he himself has not yet been, technically, seduced: hence his endless brooding. He is meant to be working but instead he walks, he takes scattered impressions, he lets his thoughts dwell. What is it that happens when repeatedly nothing happens.

The sound of footsteps makes him turn. The SEDUCER, catching up: Ah good, I thought I might find you out here. He looks very fine. His warm robes, breathtakingly expensive, are made of boiled wool in a charcoal grey. His long pale hair is tucked into the collar to stop it getting tangled on the wool. The SCHOLAR clenches his teeth briefly, trying to ignore the heavy line of all that hair. Those leather gloves he knows are lined with blue silk because he once picked one up to have a look. The SEDUCER stays just clear of fussy: elegant, yes, but more than that, he is powerful with quality and good taste. He just – this phrase recurs in all the SCHOLAR's thinking about him – he just *knows how*.

Anyway here they are – in the grounds of the SEDUCER's great estate, she decides, where the SCHOLAR is a guest. This offers the possibility of the SCHOLAR looking his friend critically up and down and remarking: How very lord of the manor.

SEDUCER: Don't you like it?

SCHOLAR: I didn't say that.

All the dialogue is like this, acidic and affectionate, equally. This constant shimmering magnetism.

They fall into step together. She holds them on either side of her mind, walking as she walks. The SCHOLAR makes no conversation, he is intently trying not to be glad to see the SEDUCER, he remembers he's meant to be exasperated. Last night came another of those straightforward, entirely *un*straightforward compliments: My friend, you are truly incomparable. Brushing the magnetic fields with a fingertip to see them twitch. Of course the SCHOLAR flushed with pleasure. But judged it necessary to take a careful twist and step out of it: I don't believe for a moment you really think that. I'm going to bed.

So now he is more nervous than usual. He stops, crouches, parts some weeds, and takes gentle hold of a plant between two fingers.

What is it? The SEDUCER's voice behind him.

The SCHOLAR turns his head half back. (She invents something rapidly.) Musk hellebore, he says.

Ah yes. A powerful aphrodisiac, am I right?

The SCHOLAR stands up in disgust, brushing earth and water off his hands: Aphrodisiacs are the only plants you seem to know about. He stalks away. The SEDUCER exhales in amusement, but also he is a little stung. He strides to catch up, already formulating how to win back his friend's goodwill.

They have been with her for years now, these two. They are in the grain of her. Naturally she hauls herself in front of her own beady eyes about them from time to time. What do they imply about her. What does it mean that they are constantly going in and out of courtyards with cloaks billowing. That the SEDUCER has a wife, of course he does, and any number of mistresses, but will happily send apologies and excuses and gifts if the opportunity arises for an evening with the SCHOLAR. And what does it mean that the SCHOLAR is unattached, that he is thin and angular, that he keeps himself wound very tight, dosing himself with concoctions of his own invention to keep his mind sharp. Every so often, perhaps once or twice a year, his body gives out and he has to sleep it off for a few weeks at the SEDUCER's house. His room there is kept ready for these occasions. The SEDUCER tends to him with infinite care, lets servants come only to the doorway, never inside. Some evenings he comes up after dinner and finds his friend fast asleep with a book splayed open on the covers. Those feverish eyes running over the pages, then falling exhausted into unconsciousness. Sometimes when she can't sleep she thinks herself into the SCHOLAR's long, limp, sleeping body, his arms curled across the thick pillows: this usually works.

And what does it mean when she inserts a version of herself into the scene, to give the SEDUCER someone to flex against, to imagine herself operated on by him. A drinks party: she knows he will be there, she has longed to meet him, his reputation has been the object of her interest for months. Now here it is, the moment of introduction. She is trembling, surely he will notice. But no. He politely shakes her hand and turns away, and that's it. Not a flicker of interest in his face. He goes back to the SCHOLAR and they stand against the wall and watch the room, like two brother princes in a gathering of lesser nobles. She is not only disappointed, she's a little humiliated, she is incredulous, she looks around with cheeks aflame. Other guests explain to each other, yes that's his good friend from the university, terribly learned you know: and the SCHOLAR thus honoured becomes a little wry and warm, a little unfurling, like a fern: and she begins to see she doesn't stand a chance.

However. In fact the SEDUCER has been keeping a light watch on her, or more precisely on her desire. When the woolly mass of it has been drawn out and twisted tight, when he is holding the end of a long stiff yarn, when she is thoroughly resigned to going home and berating herself for wanting him in the first place: *now* he appears, drink in hand. He is soft, almost hesitant, as if worried he has missed his chance, and serious, he knows he mustn't appear to be laughing at her, she is too sore for that. He asks about her research. He manages some exquisitely judged flattery. He appears, as the conversation progresses, to notice more and more of her charms. Would you like, he says, to continue this over dinner? Now her throat is tight, her head is roaring, it's really happening. Across the room is the SCHOLAR, watching them, working hard to manage his jealousy by appraising this performance against the dozens of others he's played witness to. As the SEDUCER places her coat around her shoulders and escorts her out of the room he flashes a wink at his friend. The SCHOLAR gives them a few minutes to clear the area. Then he leaves, alone.

She comes back to herself, walking by the dark river. Stops on the bank and stands against a tree, watching with the SCHOLAR's eyes. What would he see. The water endlessly filling the next space and the next space. As if desperate to stop, to rest in a pool and just move within itself, with internal currents. Where is water most comfortable. Not in a glass, exposed and helpless on all sides. Perhaps in a thick strong river, where the currents are deep and muscular. Or when it reaches the great black subterranean lakes and can vanish with relief into the dark.

Don't be like that, the SEDUCER says softly as they stand watching the water.

She holds herself as the SCHOLAR, his stiff narrow shoulders, all cut up with his unhappy affections. He doesn't answer.

The SEDUCER says, Do you want me to go?

The SCHOLAR still says nothing. Oh he can feel it's a play for forgiveness, it's fucking *laced* with tactics. But he is laced too, very tightly. All he can muster is − now how would he say this − she searches through the possibilities. Well, you're here now. Or a scornful little compliment about the SEDUCER's aesthetic contribution to the scene. Or would he just say wearily: No, stay.

She walks again. Now the SCHOLAR is examining one of the willows. Yes, look. He indicates something in the bark. It will come down this year, or next. As I understand it it's difficult to save them once they reach this stage.

The SEDUCER shakes his head: You are always telling me unpleasant truths I don't want to hear.

The SCHOLAR glances back at him, then returns his gaze to the tree. I try to do you the credit of not wasting your time. He is still having to fend off – whatever it is he is fending off. He comes back to the path and they walk on.

She has tried to creak open a door for the SCHOLAR, to allow him the simple daylight he deserves. At his college he makes a friend more like himself: the COLLEAGUE: a studious man, mild and cheerful and wry, working on something to do with, (she casts about), maybe bees, or thistles. A small friendship so far, in small gardens and courtyards only, but growing. They discuss the habits of birds, the patterns of frost on the windowpanes, the declining quality of college wine. They agree they might travel together in the summer, to look at alpine lichens.

The SEDUCER senses the new influence, he notices a new calm and brightness in his friend's face like mountain snow. He waits until the SCHOLAR is careless enough to reveal a name. Then he takes steps. Specifically he tracks the COLLEAGUE down, follows him to an inn, introduces himself, buys him something expensive to drink. Without especial difficulty seduces him. Then a few days later casually mentions it to the SCHOLAR, as if not recognising its significance. The SCHOLAR is light-headed with fury and shock, but also he knows, he *knows* it was done because of him, and he is thrilled to be guarded so fiercely. He wishes he had been there to see the game being played, to see the COLLEAGUE's expression of surprise, then suspicion, and finally helplessness. As if he has reached round with his own arm and plucked the COLLEAGUE away from himself. He wishes he wasn't enthralled by such dubious scenarios.

The next day the COLLEAGUE is shadowy faced at dinner: he meets the SCHOLAR's eye and instantly looks away. Each now knows the other knows. Oh — she gazes sadly at it — oh this is the moment when the SCHOLAR should extend a hand: Perhaps we could discuss it, it may not be the end of the world, I blame him far more than you. But he is busy sitting in his own exquisite abjection, delighted at this flatteringly proprietorial move by the SEDUCER, even enjoying an indirect triumph over the COLLEAGUE, as if to say Yes, this is the kind of friend I have, he's good, isn't he. He knows he himself is at the centre of all this. All the others have achieved is to multiply the angles.

Ah. She recognises what she has done. What is the line. Loving offenders, thus I will excuse ye. She wishes she wasn't enthralled by such dubious scenarios.

But *Rich* – stressing the word emphatically in her head, putting a new burst of momentum into her walking. She must not slip off, into verdurous glooms and winding mossy ways. Rich who is no complicated manoeuvrer: more a standard-bearer of love coming in through the front gate. But then – he is such a *presence*, such an *other person*, a thing she seems not to be good at coping with, the sheer massiveness of a whole other human. If he comes to visit everything will be different, all *this*, this chilled bright space in her head – she turns her head from side to side, mouth open feeling the brilliance of it – all this will be squashed out for a few days, covered instead with a dark blanket which is his presence. She can see how it will go. She will be angry when he does or doesn't put his hand on her waist as they walk. She will fling things at him like starfish, and he will have to peel them off. He will say something like, I thought we wanted to have a nice weekend together, and she will cry, and he will hold her, and they will waste a whole day or more while he tries to get her to accept, how did he put it before, that he *likes* her, for god's sake.

Also if he comes she will have to redistribute her chores away from Saturday and Sunday, all her grocery shopping and washing, and she won't see Bridget, and she will have to sit at her desk on Sunday night with a knot of sleep deprivation all through her throat and chest and stomach trying to read *Antony and Cleopatra* or whatever. Go to her tutorial without an essay, work into Monday evening to finish it: wake up on the Tuesday already tired, and so on. It will spill down into her week like a series of waterfalls. Other girls have boyfriends to stay: how do they find the management of it anything but intolerable, how do they—

No. She is getting boastful now: here it is in her walk, starting to swing with a kind of proud dilemma, which it needn't be. She will make the decision like normal people do, like putting a book neatly onto a shelf.

She goes back into the lane and the light changes: no longer a weak wide sunlight across everything, but blue and brown shadows with angled gleams and wedges. A small dark lawn with its allocation of snowdrops, and JESUS christ that's the chapel bell, so loud she jolts as if it has struck her full in the chest. Ten o'clock. An hour thrown on this walk, and now she really must get some work done. She turns into the cold shadowed street, and tries to understand the episode is finished.

So back into college and across the quad: briefly she is the SEDUCER striding across his own courtyard, the SCHOLAR beside him. She flickers into a comparison of their separate arrogances. The SCHOLAR depends on always being right, and usually is, and would rather say nothing than get something wrong. The SEDUCER is happy to admit he is wrong if it means he gets to be charming. But when he owns something he *really* owns it. Like this house of his. Her shoulders go back, her chin up slightly: his grey eyes like crystal are beautifully unconcerned: these stone walls are his habitat, built for his bloodline.

A couple of doors and voices – here are Robbie Fisher and Alex Grosz coming out of staircase four. She gives them a small smile, they hail her easily. Both historians, both in their boat club windbreakers, probably off for a Sunday fry-up. Alex laughs loudly at something she didn't hear, her skin tingles and shrinks, she pushes the door open into her staircase. The whole breakfast will be like that, they are good-humoured and good-looking and a bit callous, they both got scholarships when she did, they will probably get firsts and go off to do something interesting and well paid. Her legs are slightly tired going back up the stairs. Digging her key out of her pocket she palpates this idea: a scholar who is also brash, energetically brilliant, but not at all careful in ordinary conversation, swearing and generalising all over the place. Scholarship without angst.

Her room is a bright tank of warmth. She throws gloves scarf coat onto the bed, lifts the glass of water and drinks the rest, cold down her clogged throat. Goes into the bathroom to refill it and takes a look at herself. She looks better: a lifelike pinkness in her cheeks and nose. So then. That was all extremely unplanned. There was the mist, and the

SCHOLAR and SEDUCER, and the river, and her well-used legs – and whether it has been remotely helpful will now be available for judgement. She would like to believe the appreciation of beauty is never a waste. But this does not an essay write. With brute simplicity she calculates, an hour and eight minutes since she went out, so she will add an hour and eight minutes after lunch. The measurements of her routine will be thereby satisfied.

The sky is mottled blue and white now, no longer special, but she lingers at the window thinking. Robbie and Alex address each other, poshly, as *mate*. All those boys only ever hug swift and hard: no standing close, or holding tight, or cradling, or snuggling. Whereas. The image of one man stroking the velvet trim on another man's cloak. Something ringing and humming with gorgeous desire. The word *gorgeous* itself. A sliding and yes, stroking, rather than jabbing and thrusting. A low murmur. The actual sex is less interesting to her than how the ecstatic might force its way out of the unspeakable. She can hardly keep those boys apart with their brains and money and squarely cut faces and passion for alcohol – but just say: a drunken walk back from the pub, down Bear Lane or Wheatsheaf Alley, an embrace erupting out of sudden shock and blinding lust. Not implausible. A muffled but explosively pleasurable night-time hour under the sheets. Becoming a regular, secret, urbane kind of hobby. Or maybe not: one of them grins and goes back to normal, the other starts to pine and suffer.

Speaking of which: she catches herself standing there, and touches one part of her mind to another in reproof. 'Come on' she says lightly. Back to the Sonnets.

Sitting down again at her desk she checks herself through. Things still moving around in her head. Her strong walking legs have a strong walking mind attached to them which has to settle again. Also a sheer feeling like a cliff, sitting down at her desk with her lungs full of fresh air and her body a couple of miles further into the day. As if she has already conducted some business. Like a farmer coming in from the fields and barns, sitting down to drink a late morning cup of coffee and do his accounts. The satisfaction of a cup of coffee when it is thus deserved.

Ted Hughes, where did she read this, while he was at Cambridge he read a Shakespeare play between six and nine every morning. This thought hangs open like a door: for re-weighting her whole routine: a regular start to the day, to read one Shakespeare, and then a walk twice round the meadow whatever the weather, and then back for a coffee and settling into her actual work, knowing whatever else she does or doesn't produce that day, at least she has done these things. Say she started tomorrow – six days a week for another five weeks – she could just about not quite read them all before the end of term. To have still not yet read all of Shakespeare: a basic excellence she needs to get under her belt—

No. This is a familiar line. Trying to perfect her routine even further, to get even more out of each day. Like the way she used to rearrange the furniture in her bedroom at home, expecting the room suddenly to transcend its own limitations. Or like squeezing more beads onto a thread, or another brass ring around her neck to stretch it. She read somewhere about these tribeswomen in east Asia, that their necks don't actually stretch, it's the compression and reformation of the clavicle that produces the effect of length. Does the analogy hold. Yes. Yes, the routine only contains as much time as there is. Ted Hughes can please take his dark ferocity out into the corridor and stop confusing her.

But: she hauls her thoughts back inwards. Time for some deliberate thinking. Last term, finally alone with a tutor and an author, Patricia and Virginia Woolf, the first big question was, what is the correct *ethic* for reading this work? How, Patricia said, does Woolf *ask* to be read.

But, she protested, the intentional fallacy, the death of the author—

No, Patricia said, I don't mean Woolf herself, let's just cut across that – I mean the texts, what are they asking of us. How do they want us to make ourselves available to them. Or even, what are they assuming. And so then, say you just have a hunch, or a slightly vague or diffuse response to it, how do you pinpoint that, how do you turn it into critical analysis.

It was a new set of thoughts: but she felt it ripple sweetly through her leaves and branches. Immediately they agreed that Woolf asks to be read slowly, with everything activated, getting down into the texture of each word and sentence, just slow slow slow. Requiring a reader as intelligent and sensitive as the writer herself. Think, Patricia said, about the speed of her pen. The mighty inching forward of her mind.

The yawn opens up inside her, *god* she misses reading Woolf, and she gently closes it like a gate.

The Sonnets, then: also slow, like any good poem. And like any good poem they are keen to be learnt by heart and offer themselves like small jewels. The plays are dense too of course, and they can be coaxed like that, you can sit with *Twelfth Night* and painstakingly close-read – but there is more urgency, more of a pace, striding with frequent changes of direction. Turning your head quickly back and forth to follow the dialogue. It's fun, it sparkles like water, it *moves*. (It is slightly under the spell of Kenneth Branagh.)

Compared with this: staring straight down at the page at a poem. The Sonnets yawn and congeal, or rather *she* does. They are strenuous, they agonise. Even the puns and jokes have to be pushed very slowly through their holes. She takes a pen and starts to write things down. A sequence of sonnets of course is both one poem and many poems. And the typesetting is important. George Eld the miserly printer of 1609 squashed them right up together, not even a single line break, just the number of the next one and straight in. Literally mid-page the sequence swerves from the Young Man to the Dark Lady. Whereas this genteel modern edition gives each one its own spread: notes on the left and the sonnet on the right, suspended in white space like a silent, double-glazed room. Poems that are in the world, and poems that aren't.

What else. Some of them are openly sequential, following straight on from one another to develop a set of arguments. Others are what, amnesiac? disingenuous? not acknowledging the extent of their repetitions, of the sheer grossness of his effort. He flits around his subject, a small bird working over the same network of branches every day. Or he crouches like a burglar holding a stethoscope to a safe, turning the wheel one notch at a time, hardly breathing, listening for the moment when everything clicks together and the door swings open and his hands are flooded with rubies.

Ah: she has moved away from valid information. Where did she – yes, *amnesiac*, that is a useful thought, she writes the word down and circles it. She also writes down *disingenuous*, and then also *sly*, and *defiant*.

He is dead, remember. No idea why she's thinking this, but. He rebukes and complains and boasts again and again about death, and now he really is dead. Creeping and crawling with obsession, and now dead.

Say – another scene begins to unspool: say the young man, the real one, finally comes to the Globe to see a play. He has read a lot of those sonnets, yes yes very witty very on-the-nose, very boringly aimed at himself, but he's never seen any of Will's stuff on the stage, and heaven knows the old man has begged him for so long to come and watch. He turns up one afternoon and pays his entrance: at least this will be a favour bestowed, or a debt discharged.

And then? He begins to watch. He begins *really* to watch. Sitting on his tuppenny cushion he forgets, while also intensely knowing, that it's Will down there in that costume, these are Will's words the players are speaking. He laughs when everyone laughs. Then he catches himself realising, holy mother of god, Will Shakespeare is a man bone-and-blood in the theatre, this has been the truth of it all along. (That phrase *all along*: the glitter of revelation.) He thinks, why can't I have known this Will first, how have I had the misfortune to snare the dreary sonneteer not this swaggering King's Man. Down on the boards Will is dividing things up into spaces of lust and loyalty – he walks over here with this line, and turns it back with a hand gesture – he delivers a stinging insult to a blushing woman – with a few words he makes another man look at him sharply in a moment of sudden stillness – or he makes that distance, *this* distance, thrum with bewildered longing. Heaven and earth, this is what the old man wanted him to come and see: he knew exactly what he was doing.

Then in the tavern afterwards he meets Will's mistress. He is decidedly on the back foot now, he didn't even know about the mistress, but, well, he is still a man and she is just a woman. He proves his own obscure point to himself: he seduces her. Early next morning a hungover fleshy-faced Will crawls to his desk and squeezes out a few miserably brilliant sonnets. Small consolation for waking up without either of them.

She pauses thinking. There is a tiny urge in her cunt like a lit match. She considers it: it burns steadily. She could, she *could*, unbutton her jeans right now and add a new entry to her ledger of masturbatory self-interruptions. She really shouldn't, especially after that unscheduled walk, but. Thinking again about those boys pressed against the wall in an alleyway, each with a hand deep in the other's trousers. Fingertips brushing against the twitching length of an erection. Yes.

Maybe if she slid a pen down into the tight space between fabrics where her hand won't fit. She has done. Continued to work feeling it snugly promisingly there against her knickers. Managed maybe twenty minutes more before taking herself to lie on the bed, or remaining at the desk began to twist and slide the pen to get little tweaks around her clitoris. But it's a commitment of time: of which she has already wasted plenty today. She would rather not come at all than end up sullen and unsatisfied from a runty orgasm she didn't bother to build up. The things she does, she does properly. Painstakingly finds them out anew every time. Which strand of fantasy will make good today. Sometimes she goes partway down a certain route before abandoning it for something else. Or roams and shuffles through images, gestures, phrases, tempting herself with variety: this can work in the early phase, all the possible excitements: but she has to commit, to develop one idea fully, in the end. It is not unlike choosing a book to buy from a very good bookshop.

Her orgasms have species, and families. The feeble impatient one which hovers and flutters briefly, then diffuses itself through her cunt and is gone: just about good enough for getting to sleep, but that's all. The solid, well-deserved

73

one, carefully constructed, it thumps in her a few times, announcing itself with drums. Then there is an unusual one, arrived at swiftly but if, say, it's been a while, it comes like a jolt of light through her cunt, it knocks her into a surprise *ahh!* gasp. Her wild fleshy parts down there in the dark with their own rhythms and reactions.

The best and strangest ones are those infused from the beginning with a feeling of deliciousness. Often in the middle of the day like this, when she is meant to be doing something else. Spending some time *preparing* to take herself across the room to lie down on the bed, the slowly revolving knowledge of yes that's what we're going to do, she feels it taking shape, she and a dirty gleeful part of her brain snuggle together and watch, satisfied with her naughtiness. She might be wet long before anything begins officially. These ones just involve following the scent of it in her mind, there is no leading or selecting or deciding. There are things she will do to herself in this state. And then when she comes it's like a chunk of glacier collapsing into the sea, with vertigo and shockwaves and catastrophic melting. Then everything very still and grey: she has reached the bottom of her own barrel.

Oh, she could. But, she takes a long breath, no, she won't.

Anyway shouldn't she be thinking about Rich these days. Which is a different genus, a different class even: you have to close one book and open another, no longer fish but now ferns, or something. With him she is less interested in the orgasm, it seems too fussy and specific to bother with. Other things become available. Put simply, she likes being fucked. She likes the degree and direction of force he can put through her, how high up in her pelvis he can get. The penis turgid with blood: belonging in the same category as the sperm whale which, when it wants to dive, densifies the gloop in its head into a white waxy solid. How liquid can be so *stiff*. And his entering gasps as the slick stretched latex pushes into her, his noises containing an implication of Ohhh finally, or Christ yes this is what I've needed. Pleasure, she read somewhere, is antisocial, can only be spectated, not shared. Yes. She can meet his eyes with enjoyment, he can look at her panting and smiling, but she is just watching his short transfixing drama of relief, while conducting her own separate fervour as he thumps into her. Then they come back and are drowsy and whimpering together.

Her legs have twisted themselves tightly around each other like tree branches. For god's sake. Whatever happened to her plan of being celibate. *Radically* celibate was how she put it to herself. Grey-eyed Athene, watching over her with satisfaction, infusing her with that same warm satisfaction. Yet here she is, can't even get through a morning without frizzing herself up like this.

She takes a mouthful of cold water and rolls it around her tongue and teeth, drawing the heat out of them. Actually she wants more coffee: the mechanism is thrumming in her brain. Of course she knows, Annabel you know perfectly well, how coffee only makes everything better until it doesn't, until it abruptly decides it's finished and pulls the plug. Dull sluggish and stupid would be the result she absolutely doesn't need. She will hold out. If she can make it to lunch it will be acceptable that coffee is over for the day.

Somewhere outside a dove is sighing rhythmically into the bright air. She starts to twist her pen between her fingers, registering again the poem in front of her and her page of sparse notes. Feels like an hour ago she wrote down this word *defiant*.

A master of silence could spend a lifetime accommodating himself to the way different breezes go through a single willow tree. All she is doing here is pushing tiny pins into a tiny board and winding them thick with her own threads. That's really all.

A small lift in her mind: could she write about *punctuation* in the Sonnets? Specifically, all the things that are spoilt or at least altered when the pointing is changed by a modern editor, all the extra commas and semicolons jammed into the lines, clogging up the swinging flexible feel of them. She imagines for a moment an essay that knows all the subtleties of Jacobean printing conventions, traces beautifully how thoughts are lightly directed and compartmentalised by the original punctuation, and expresses with elegant sorrow the loss of this finesse in pedantic modern editions. A loss of flow, yes, a loss of swagger. Also something about colons: which in the Sonnets sometimes simply mark the end of quatrains, without the performance of anticipation a colon carries now. She thinks of psalms, she sees dimly how the remit of the colon has been reduced over the centuries. But after all this is not exactly about the Sonnets. Suspects herself somewhat of laziness. Poems are there to be *read*, not combed through for evidence: a mass of hair to be brushed into a deep shine, not to have nits brought out of it.

But there is so little *time* here, an undergraduate degree is so hyperactive and glancing. She has three days total to research and write her whole Sonnets essay. Plenty of topics are therefore outside the penumbra of the possible. She cannot write about the Sonnets' connections to other sonnet sequences, to other Shakespeare plays, to historical context. Or real-life candidates for the Young Man or the Dark Lady, or the authority for printing, or the vagaries of the sequencing. She needs something sharp, like a dagger: to slip in and quickly out again.

It might be laptop time. Dictionary time. Concordance

time. Time to skim a few articles at random and find something to bounce off.

She gets up and goes over to the shelf and brings back her laptop to her desk. Plugs it in and switches it on. Makes a grim 'Hmm' as the screen comes alight: her standard greeting for her laptop. As it grinds through its start-up routine it officiously shows her different screens and progress bars, to persuade her of its competence. She stands there, suddenly thinking of Rich's broad body. His thick forearms with their sweep of hair. Putting her hand on his forearm and grasping it lightly. Then reaching further and taking hold of his belt buckle. The clink of the belt parts detaching from each other and the leather sliding out, god she loved that, it panged between her legs, and he moaned too seeing her undress him, the way he always moans at anything she does to him unsolicited, he construes it as the overpowering of her natural reticence by her too-fierce desire. And then his cock: so sensitive that a blow job has to be just a series of gentle wet mouthings. Once the foreskin is down she must keep her mouth on him, she can't release him to the air or he gasps in pain and grabs to cover himself up. But worth getting it right, to hear him. The beauty, the agony, of a man finally sliding off the anchorage of himself.

Perhaps she and Rich will get married and live quietly and he can build his medical career and she can do a DPhil on Shakespeare or Woolf. Somewhere in the middle they will meet and give physick to each other. That unspeaking delight sometimes between them, when they look into each other's faces: serious, and delighted. Also true that nothing in even the best of the Sonnets can convincingly replicate the sensation of being fucked by him. What if she kept her words over here, and her body and smiles for Rich. Seems as good an arrangement as could be found for her.

She flashes a look at the window and the window flashes back an image of high blue skies which tempts her for a moment with the tip of itself, the smiling hints of spring, until she says quietly 'None of that' and turns back to her desk, sits down at her laptop. Now she must be strict with herself. She knows how this can go: a kind of stepping-stone technique, jumping from screen to screen making decisions too quickly, reading a paragraph here and there, following references through dark twisting passageways: no longer concerned with seeing the whole field, just following a single point of light over the horizon.

Her laptop is ready to cooperate. She clicks and types and within two minutes is elbow-deep in articles about the Sonnets.

She reads about sincerity, literal and imaginative.

She enjoys the word *sonneteer*.

She wonders briefly how the verb *emend* relates to the verb *amend*, thinks about looking it up in the dictionary, does not.

She reads about the safety of sonnet-writing, compared to love-declaring. Considers whether the safety of all lyric poetry is just another way of describing loneliness. Seems too large and terrible a thought to write down.

She remembers girls at school when they were doing Keats: complaining, that to pick these poems apart was a way of spoiling them, sucking out all the joy and wonder.

(The way they could make laziness look like extraordinary sensitivity to beauty.)

Miss Francis listened patiently and said Hmmm and then turned: Annabel, Tilda, what do you think? Because it was established by this point that she and Tilda were both going to Oxford to read English. This pushed their class a bit out of shape, in a way Miss Francis seemed to find useful. She appealed to them more. Put another way, she let them do more of the work.

She, Annabel, considered by way of answer simply reciting 'Ode to a Nightingale'. All eighty lines. Obviously too much like showing off. Instead she said No, it's like, a different kind of beauty, when you know it really well. At that time she was realising more and more the gulf between how well she thought and how poorly she spoke.

Tilda was much more articulate and said something about how you had to put the poem back together again after taking it apart.

But how do you do that, Samantha protested, how do you forget all the stuff about enjambment and metaphors and things.

Tilda shrugged.

Miss Francis stepped back in: Wait until after the exam before you do any forgetting please Samantha.

Yes, the Annabel answer would certainly have been Learn it by heart. Probably adding somewhat dramatically, It's the only way. Keep it close, wear it right next to your skin. So lines come to you at odd times. You can sit hungover on the train and think sleepily about the sad heart of Ruth

81

when sick for home she stood in tears amid the alien corn. And see how standing in tears in the middle of a field is desperately sadder than sitting in tears on the sofa at home.

The other hard answer she could have flicked across the table like a coin: Why the hell are you doing English A Level then.

She finds, in Helen Vendler:

> A theory of critical reading might begin: Know your texts for decades. Recite many of them to yourself so often that they seem your own speech. Type them out, teach them, annotate them. A critical 'reading' is the end product of an internalisation so complete that the word *reading* is not the right word for what happens when a text is on your mind. The text is part of what has made you who you are.

This paragraph reaches a certain threshold in her mind. She gets up and fetches the small notebook from her bedside drawer, copies the whole thing out, and puts the notebook away.

The final mystery of the work, how things went in and connected and came out as ten-syllable lines rhyming and intertwining again and again – this is finally the thing her essay will fling itself against and dissolve like foam.

All over Oxford this year's batch of undergrads is sitting in rooms and libraries making exactly the same flinging and dissolving movements. Trying to comprehend how a man called – of all the things to be called, honestly – William Shakespeare – a man called William Shakespeare who presumably like everyone else was afraid of everything – how he sat and wrote with his actual hand, on actual paper, the words that have become a *text*.

In her mind a little pocket of grief springs open and disperses like seeds: he is dead, he is dead, dead dead dead dead dead, and it falls into the grass.

Actually the SCHOLAR is still here with her, just lightly. Here is his antisocial texture, his weariness with anything except the work. He comprehends all these parts of her: he is comprehensive.

He however *is* working, and she is not.

She continues to read.

In William Empson she finds, to her pleasure, that Elizabethan poets revelled in the casualness of commas, the reader makes up the logic of the phrases for himself, the phrases go either way. Something about *going either way*: yes, exactly: she writes this down.

She reads about the especial *virility of content* in the English sonnet tradition: resists it: then remembers she had a not dissimilar thought.

She puts the word *shame* into the Shakespeare concordance, she looks at all the places he has mentioned shame, she finds a couple of articles and realises there is a muscular history and theory of shame that she would need weeks to think herself into. She abandons this line.

She reads in Eve Kosofsky Sedgwick that: for a man to undergo even a humiliating change in the course of a relationship with another man still feels like preserving or participating in a sum of male power, while for a man to undergo any change in the course of a relationship with a woman feels like a radical degeneration of substance.

Yes. *Yes.* This is why the SEDUCER tends to prefer a simple evening with the SCHOLAR to even the most febrile bed-session with a woman, any woman. And this is why the SCHOLAR allows his pattern of solitude, slow work, contemplation, to be burst into by these dark-glowing hours with the SEDUCER, and then still inwardly glittering goes back to his books and hammers and exerts until he's cold and hard again. She nods slowly. Yes if he is so seemingly independent it's because he has one presiding, cardinal dependence, like creeping roots under the soil, like the ground elder in the garden at home: hardy, invasive, patch-forming. And if it weren't this it would only be something else, larger doses of his homemade stimulants, or a new infatuation with no established protocol, a ravaging kind of novelty. He has calculated it to be safer to let the existing coloniser stay, rather than trying to expel him and opening the ground for a new, unforeseen tyrant.

Ah. She lets her head drop forward, feels the pull in the snug muscles of her neck. Another lapse into her own realm. Some of this comes from the Sonnets, they are spreading again, they are overlapping in her mind with the SCHOLAR's crystalline obsession: which is really *her* crystalline obsession, grown from a saturated solution over many years. This is the thing about sonnet sequences, they are so personal they are either cold or queasy. (She writes this down.)

Or perhaps crystal is the wrong image: perhaps instead long dark fronds growing up from the depths of it, or from her own depths. She draws a few fronds, not very good ones, in the margin of her paper. They reach up, they drag down.

If she can write this essay she will be like a small snail successfully climbing a blade of grass. She will see clearly perhaps twelve or fifteen more blades of grass around her, and beyond that an undifferentiated mass of green, and above her the summery darkness which she vaguely understands to be trees. Climbing other blades of grass on other days she will become familiar with how each differs in angle, breadth, hue, curvature. They will vary so extremely as to barely belong in the same category, or else the categories will proliferate to the point of uselessness. This then is scholarship. And a great careful lifetime of reading might give simply a sense of the grass growing a little higher towards that vast unreachable canopy. She could write to Helen Vendler and ask her, really, honestly, is it worth it, has it made you more contented, or just more aching?

Maybe if it rained. Sometimes a dark day of rain is more of a comfort than all the reading and yoga and meditation of a whole week. Rain falls calmly and sensibly and leaves her alone.

Her own concentration is starting to unhinge now. She tries to work on it: no touching her hair or crossing or uncrossing her legs or murmuring to herself. To make only deliberate movements to lift her glass to her mouth, not just sprinkle them carelessly like sand through the work. Again the image of herself brown and still, sitting in perfect concentrated suspension in a warm courtyard. Everything with a poise, a clarity.

Anyway she reads as patiently as possible. When she catches herself drifting she patiently returns to it. But no clear sign of improvement yet. Some days she can't get through even a whole sentence and fucking hell is it even worth it this whole golden circus of knowledge, and she has to catch and cradle all these angry crinkling parts of herself. Can get into a sorry state this way. She is not a natural scholar, there, that is the truth, she tries to tame her choppy mind but bits of foam come flying off the surf, this sitting-thinking-reading isn't her best aspect. Be damned the series of historical moves which created reading as a stationary activity. She wants to be walking all day. Her mind goes quiet along the river, along the field-edge path, across the rainy expanse of Port Meadow, or it's like, the scraps and gusts become a steady and throughflowing breeze. She walks, and hot insight cools into a silent wisdom. But in what way that helps: well, in point of fact it doesn't help. There is no writing it down. It's *vaporous*, or is *volatile* the word: it lifts out of her without so much as a by-your-leave and returns to the grass, the trees, the water. It produces only a longing for more of the same, it creates an effect, that seems to be all. She can't pick up earth from the ground and eat it.

Anyway she has to sit and so. If she can thicken her own

concentration now she won't have to be fighting herself her whole career. An exhausting thought, of clenching her brain over a book, every day for ever and ever.

What she wants, what she has perhaps (in her most admitting to herself moments) conceived him for in the first place, is the SCHOLAR's massive endurance: his brain fixed upon the page, absolutely intent and still, travelling evenly and slowly through each sentence. An occasional twitch in his mind which indicates he has not quite understood something, as if the brain-fibres were drawing together briefly in puzzlement, and he goes back and reads the sentence again: usually a second time is enough. Every so often, when something occurs to him, or simply at the end of a paragraph, he raises his head to take a long cool drink of air and thought. He might write a small thing down, most often a question. Then locks his mind back into the dense absorbing text. Stays in this attitude, taking only water and coffee, for hours at a time. Does not fidget, or get up to stoke the fire or add more logs, or open or shut the window. Does not even stop to question whether he is really paying attention: is entirely unselfconscious about it: just *works*.

Pressing on towards midday. There is a very faint warmth coming through the windows, the sun is making excellent progress across its low portion of sky. She isn't. She hasn't worked well and she is getting hungry. Here is the page of her notebook with a few half-developed sentences, the only thoughts she has been able to lay down. Partly the walk, the mist and meadow and water, and the SCHOLAR and SEDUCER: she has lived too much of her own existence already today to fully commit to what's happening in these poems. Shouldn't have swerved into whimsical scene-making so early in the day when she needed her mind to be sitting bolt upright. And they are irreversibly in the Sonnets now, the SCHOLAR and SEDUCER. She has rubbed them in, like butter into flour. Contaminating and cross-pollinating these two angsty couples. Cannot be helped, but: she murmurs aloud 'What – am – I – doing.'

Studying the Sonnets ought to bring out the best in all literature students: smiling in recognition of subtlety. This phrase sounds like a quote, but who knows where from, and she writes it down unattributed. Could an essay smile with all the smiles she has for the Sonnets: the sad smile of sympathy, the wry smile sharing in his self-mockery, the raised-eyebrow smile detaching from him when he gets too ridiculous, the soft sunlit smile when he offers an image of great beauty. She notices: no smiles of actual amusement. The Sonnets are not funny, when the plays are so often oh my god hilarious. Could *that* be an essay. She writes it down. Compared to the ravenous, jeering crowd of the theatre: the sonnet's narrow room, where one can hole up and take oneself extremely seriously.

~

She thinks of Miles. (A real person living and breathing! She smiles: a faint smile.) How will he be getting on with the Sonnets. Is their blankness the right kind of blankness for him. He likes Shelley, the most difficult kind of blank she's ever read, so perhaps he will find the Sonnets positively *bristling*. They might in their squeezing overwhelm him: for he is all faded like someone has turned his colour saturation down, with his quiet quick voice, like every time the air through his vocal cords catches him slightly by surprise.

Carefully she places her mind onto the memory of that friendship last year. They started to stop for tea on the way back from tutorials. They told each other about their sisters. His long fingers wrapped around his warm cup. He smiled small smiles, but smiled them easily. She expected it to broaden into, well, it was spring and the days themselves were broadening into summer, and they talked about Austen and why he liked *Mansfield Park*, and they shared a distrust of Blake, and he said with complete self-determination he would do Wordsworth for his special author. Many quiet conversations. And in the quad late at night there was one long hug, before he turned to walk home to his shared house, and she ascended overjoyed to her room.

In the vast sunlight on May Morning they went together to hear the choir on the tower. Only nine months ago, but she has to grip with her mind, trying in this shrivelled winter light to remember the brilliance of summer. Everything full of leaves and birds, and crowds of people pouring towards Magdalen at ten to six. After the singing they wandered through the streets, saw the Morris dancers, astonished accepted free coffee from a leafy-branch-covered man with an urn strapped to his back. She made a light mocking comment about Morris dancing, and Miles didn't laugh but watched the dancers carefully, and said, Is it – I wonder if it could be a class thing, do you think. She realised he was trying to challenge her as mildly as possible, he didn't want to humiliate her. She tried to see what he saw. He explained: he was trying to be on the lookout for where his tastes had been influenced by his upbringing. Like garden gnomes, loathed by his own parents but clearly very popular with many people. (He didn't specify his own position on garden gnomes.) She nodded, and then saw something in the Morris dancing all green and white, and followed him to the maypole where ribbons were being danced into tight patterns, and saw things in that too. He was far more advanced than her: her thoughts curled up on that cushion while she stood next to him not speaking.

Descendants of those thoughts come to her now. His mind is wide and clear like a sea breeze. He will be having no trouble with the Sonnets.

Anyway it never did broaden, because suddenly he had a girlfriend, Katie Kitchener, a small bright girl in the year below, doing English and Classics. She hadn't ever seen them talk. Now they were together all the time, in T-shirts and sunglasses in the garden, or heads bent over their books side by side in the library. Even seven months later she rarely sees one without the other. And thankfully, or intolerably, her tutorial pairings this year have gone every which way but him. She hasn't spoken to him on his own since, well, they had a chat in October about their summer holidays, speaking in their old quiet way outside the library, and then after a few minutes Katie appeared and Miles's arm lifted to wrap round her shoulders, and while she looked on

Katie was smiling with frank happiness, apparently seeing no reason why she shouldn't. She, Annabel, went back up to her room and sat very still, and then made herself as a solemn treat a cup of strong coffee with lots of hot milk.

There was a moment when her pen hovered over the Wordsworth box, before moving up and putting a firm tick next to Woolf.

That Trinity Term she was just starting to bring her mornings earlier and earlier. Again she tries to think of summer: *Trinity* a word with so much light in it: daylight when she woke up, daylight still when she went to bed. She could pad around the room in her bare feet and pyjamas, sit lightly down and read a poem, get up and look out the window, sit down again and reread it. There was a burst of good weather and every morning when she woke up there was birdsong and a cool golden light in her room. Then she would get out of bed no matter how early it was and go quietly to her desk, or pull a jumper on and go down into the garden, enjoying how warm and snuggled everyone else was, all the bodies up there in their beds like long feet in socks, and then her own small wet feet getting cold in the grass and picking up dust in the quad and drying out on the rough carpeted stairs and ready to brush off by the time she reached her door. The shadows were all sharp and vivid in the two big trees, one bright green beech and one bright green oak, there was a rippling cool shadow over her, she got her hand wet in the grass and wiped it over her face. And maybe she had dreamed something physical and memorable about a grown man, his good grip. Going back to her room destabilised in a kind of green and white euphoria.

So it began to be that six o'clock was the latest she would set her alarm, and often she would get up earlier still. This made it necessary to give up somewhat on evenings. She pottered about in her room as the light took its leave, put on her bedside lamp, changed and brushed her teeth, got into bed and managed maybe fifteen minutes of reading. When she turned off the lamp there was blue light coming in from outside, and some birds still singing. At these times she lay very quiet and listened, and rested.

She pauses. Her hunger is a fixed pang in her stomach now, weakening her whole body, like someone has nailed through her strength. She has a bit of a shake on. Normally she would stop at midday: no way she can do that today: but nor can she continue sitting here like this. Perhaps a break for lunch, a slow thinking lunch, and then try again in an hour or so.

Rumi says:

There's hidden sweetness in the stomach's emptiness. . .
If the brain and the belly are burning clean
with fasting, every moment a new song
comes out of the fire.

She leans back slightly from this, but also thinks about it often. Somewhere she has read that it is possible to live on significantly less food than we all assume, and that this produces a cleaner, lighter existence. Her mind aspiring to the fluency of a cool spring river. But how to get down from a stodgy two thousand calories a day she hasn't yet discovered. All conscious attempts to eat less have ended the same: wolfing bread and butter in the afternoon of the third or fourth day. She is suited for regulation not reduction, something like that.

Anyway it turns out she is getting up from her chair and stretching. Her body pretending to respond to a command she never actually gave it. Well, all right. A gathering of nutritious foodstuffs into a good and wholesome lunch.

As she leaves her desk there is another slight stretch: herself leaving her mind, leaving the text, leaving the realm of poetic infatuation. She becomes the SCHOLAR for a few seconds, conceding to hunger after a long morning of work, giving a slow exhale as he stands up straight, lifts his arms above his head, and takes his slender self through to the larder, as she picks up a bowl and a sharp knife and puts the door on the latch and steps out of her room—

—and a sudden image comes, her mind making a small lunchtime gift, of the SCHOLAR not in his usual black robes but in blue jeans, a loose shirt, a dark ponytail – what he might be like in Rome, say, going out in the early morning to drink coffee – he takes long easy strides across the piazza, he does and doesn't know how gorgeous he is, he does and doesn't see the looks of admiration—

Anyway here she is in the empty kitchen. She opens the fridge and sees that yet again her orange Sainsbury's bags have been moved to a different shelf. In their place is Emma's food: mostly half-finished packets of tomatoes and smoked salmon – next to Grace's food: a neat row of three apples and two pots of low-calorie soup – above Bill's food: a packet of coffee clipped shut and an unopened wedge of brie – next to Sanjay's food: a Tupperware of leftovers, a bottle of milk a week out of date, a half-empty bottle of wine.

She pulls her bags out and shuts the fridge. Opens the bags and peers in. Nothing is obviously missing. What gets stolen are things that don't come in numbers: coffee, alcohol, milk, occasionally cheese. Never vegetables. These days she scores in biro the line of the milk and leaves that side facing out: just you dare.

∾

She arrays celery, cucumber, tomatoes, parsley, a packet of mozzarella. Levers two sticks of celery out from the base, brushes some dirt off them under the tap, lays them down, takes the knife and positions the blade in the inside curve of one stick: then slices it from end to end in one careful motion. Repeats with the other. The brief joy of the knife: if only more things were like the efficient sharp action of a knife through cellulose, feeling each fibre give to the blade edge. The pile of parsley begins to crumple under the strokes of the knife, turning from plants to an ingredient, a rough handful of chopped fresh herbs. Then cucumber, wetly and easily sliced, and six cherry tomatoes, each one given an individual attention, righted with the little dent on top to give the knife a point of purchase. This knife is not good: it *splits* rather than *severs* the tomato skin, it's an effortful spurting execution not a gentle instantaneous one. At home her preferred knife is bigger-bladed and will cut goat's cheese for instance or banana simply with its own weight. Its sharpness holds its own mini-legendary space in her mind.

She snips the corner off the mozzarella packet, drains the cloudy water into the sink, and cuts it fully open, releasing the ball of cheese onto the chopping board in a thin puddle of liquid. Seems inaccurate for the same knife to chop this as well as the plants. Nevertheless. Something comes back – the SCHOLAR, lean in his black shirt, shaking out the day's newspaper and taking a swift drink of espresso – as she uses her whole hands to gather up the wet pieces of cheese and drops them into the bowl on top of the vegetables. Then carving open the tins of lentils and chickpeas, half a tin each dumped into the sieve and rinsed under a gush of cold water and into the bowl too. She taps the sieve to knock the clinging lentils off the mesh. The food gleams in its bowl—

The door opens and here is Sanjay, his hair puffed up, in a T-shirt and pyjama bottoms. 'Hey' he says dully, crouching down to open the fridge.

'Hi' she says, watching him rummage.

'*Fuck*' he says in conclusion and thumps the fridge door shut.

She chooses not to respond to this. He smells strangely good – aftershave, cigarette smoke, sweat – a whole tangle of living bodily smells. Now he is leaning his head into his hands on the counter. 'Your lunch looks unbelievably fucking healthy' he says in a muffled voice.

She laughs. 'You're feeling unwell I'm guessing.'

He groans. 'You probably don't even get hangovers do you' he says 'you're so fucking radiant with health, you probably don't even *drink*.'

'Maybe not as much as you' she says smiling.

He opens the fridge door and looks again. 'Do you think Grace would mind if I had one of her soups?'

'Probably' she says. Already suspecting what he will say next.

'Is she even going to eat it herself' he says shutting the fridge. 'I mean it's not like, you know.'

Yes, that. She shrugs. 'You're welcome to some of my stuff if you want.'

'Thanks' he says, but it's more of a moan, and he's already going out of the kitchen again.

She assesses her own behaviour. Dignified yes, generous yes. Notes that she felt permitted to laugh at him because it's a hangover: if he had been genuinely ill she would have been sympathetic. Oh he smelled wonderful. Honestly if he had asked her to come and get into bed with him—

'No not that' she says aloud. Instead she gives the moment to the SEDUCER: unshaven, the worse for wear, he joins the SCHOLAR at breakfast and mutters How the hell do you look so unscathed. The SCHOLAR smiles faintly: the fine point of seldom pleasure.

The corridor is warmer than the kitchen. Pushing back into her room she finds it warmer again. She puts the bowl full of texture and colour down on her low table. Now a little olive oil, salt, pepper. Mixes carefully with her shining spoon. Sits down in her low chair to eat.

Thinking now about *compliments*: the trickiness of them, the performance of them. Certainly from Sanjay's remarks, which she did not find especially complimentary. Maybe also from the Sonnets, the dubious nature of the poet's compliments. Indeed the dubious nature of *all* compliments. As Rumi says:

What the sayer of praise is really praising is
himself, by saying implicitly,
'My eyes are clear.'

And therefore the dubious nature of Rich's compliments: you have such an incredible memory, your hair looks gorgeous like that, I really do admire your dedication. That is: look at me, look at what I have meticulously noticed, see how piercingly I catalogue you.

The food is wet and crunchy, and tastes of all the cutting-up she just did to it. A poetics, then, of compliments. As in the Sonnets: Thou best of dearest, and mine only care – ah, no, this is not a compliment, not really. What else. Gentle thou art, and therefore to be won. Beauteous thou art, therefore to be assailed. Time's best jewel. Et cetera. If I remark upon what I cannot access, you will see how my longing is in fact entirely clear-sighted, sinewy and valuable with thought. And what is't but mine own when I praise thee.

A scene in which the SCHOLAR and SEDUCER, each being

interested in his own and the other's vanity, exchange compliments of extreme precision and specificity, all stuffed with implication.

SEDUCER: You are so still, even when you're moving, you're never fidgety or hectic, you always seem to carry an aura of calm with you: (that is, I recognise and applaud in you what I have never tried to cultivate in myself).

SCHOLAR: You always give extremely good presents: (that is, I am always pleased by how well you know me).

SEDUCER: You listen so well, you give such a high quality of attention to people: (mainly, that is, to me).

SCHOLAR: My impression is that you never make your lovers feel idiotic or ashamed for wanting you: (not that I would know).

When she has cleaned all the food out of the bowl into her mouth, she fetches the packet of almonds from its shelf and peels it open. Sitting *at her leisure* – this phrase lands in her lap – she picks out one almond at a time and eats it.

Really is it ever possible to find a speech which is truly humble. A way of speaking not straddled tightly by one's ego. For instance, how should one reply when being corrected on a mistake. Like in last week's tutorial when Jamie mixed up Prince Hal and Harry Hotspur, and Jonathan had to put him right. Ought it to be

Oh yes, of course, that's right: (in fact I knew that all along and I verify the accuracy of your correction). Or

Ohhhh, OK right yes: (I am completely able to assimilate what you have just said, my error before was merely a small miscalculation). Or

Oh, really? I never knew that: (I am surprised, not because the information is itself surprising, but because I ought to have known it, by virtue of knowing so much already).

She takes a celery stick into her mouth and bites off a chunk. God almighty is there any mode of conversation which isn't just a bolstering of oneself. Even expressing sympathy: see, *see*, I have noticed your suffering. The fibres of the celery spread around her mouth and creep stringily towards her gag reflex, and she fights to bring them back. How does anyone ever manage to talk to anyone. This is why silence. Jamie's reaction was an unhappy pause – Oh, he said – right – and he went a little red. Most truthful of all.

A single almond splinters and disperses among her molars. This is bad now, about the Sonnets. She still has nothing. She will have to push her routine even further back, work far into the afternoon, trawl ever more desperately for ideas. Could she, she flickers a smile, could she provocatively write an essay about her own failure to write an essay. Would the tutorial eyebrows raise.

What would the SCHOLAR do. (He can make himself useful, since he is still hanging about.) He would probably reject the short-term knowledge demanded by the essay deadline. He would read the Sonnets intensely for a week, perhaps two, and if he still had no ideas by then would be content with the intimacy his reading had afforded, he would trust it to reveal itself over time and attach itself to new things. Three almonds later and now she has to poke her tongue around for all the trapped bits niggling against her gums. Yes the SCHOLAR would consider an undergraduate degree a waste of time: flicking his brain momentarily against something he'll only have to come back to later on. He doesn't bother to learn something unless he can commit *really* to learn it. The phrase that best describes him, (one she tries not to snuggle into,) is *private scholarship*. Study undertaken for its own sake, with no deadlines, no projected outcomes. Its motives, movements, machinery, all are inward and evolving. Following a butterfly across a field, accompanying its intensive dithering, with no net.

With a heave of breath she comes back again into the room. Nearly one o'clock. Time to move. The lunch break is always tricky: so easy to sink into the pale yellow drift of the afternoon, or to try and accomplish fiddly little emails or tidying up. She should turn her phone on and see what of the world is waiting for her.

She goes to the window and looks out. The dark bare tree branches and flowerbeds, coated in weak sunlight. Beyond that the wet masses of meadow. The year has turned. Mid-winter is always a time for deep personal seeking and testing. Gawain leaves the drowsy warmth of the castle and rides terrified into the dead frozen wilderness to find the Green Chapel. And Ged sails to the furthest reaches of Earthsea, past the last islands, to seek out and confront his shadowy enemy. This part of the year, the darkest most private time, it has its own dimension. Like an upland loch, remote and unvisited, surrounded by hills which do not recognise the day when one year tips into the next. Against this vastness humans always fail to understand, always require mercy.

She thinks about New Year's Day. The four of them standing in a row on the beach, teeth chattering and steam whirling off their coffee. They all woke freezing cold in the dark in a huddle of sleeping bags, Mum wrestled her-self into her leggings and went off for a run along the waterline, the three sisters lay talking in the dark for a bit and were outside by the time Mum came back, Annabel getting the stove going for coffee and Sophy and Caroline chasing around trying to get warm. Once the day was well established, and two seals had dipped their heads up and been wished a happy new year and gone off nonplussed down the coast, they struck the tent and loaded the car and found the *Goldberg Variations* CD, and she offered to drive and Mum said no she felt fine, and the car started on the second try, and they set off. Sophy and Caroline slept. Mum drove in her own private Bach silence. She herself looked out the window at the new year spreading itself across the land.

She turns back to the room and gathers everything up, the two bowls, the two spoons wiped in straight lines between her lips, the cafetière with its uneven layer of wet dark coffee, and the small brown mug which she hooks over her little finger. Holding it all in a careful arrangement she manoeuvres the door open and steps cleanly out into the corridor. Yes, the year has turned. *Cloudez vplyften*. The Gawain-poet's description of spring goes on for several lines, but these two words do everything. It comes like a breath. Soon in a matter of weeks it will be early spring, *dark* spring as she thinks of it, fresh and wet and Lenten, when all the fields and branches are still black and only occasional bushes are white with blossom, and the weather stumbles painfully from wind and rain to splitting raw sunlight. There is relief, but also anxiety, now everything is compelled to grow and flower and build and breed and this all requires endurance, intensity, exertion without cease: and yet the idea of spring is so intoxicating that the stressful shrieking of territory is interpreted as, of all things, *song*.

In the kitchen she places everything in the sink, turns to dump the coffee grounds into the bin, and opens the hot tap. Right: being realistic now, about this essay. Say an hour of very concentrated work, just select a few sonnets to analyse in intensive detail. The sink fills with water and foam and steam. Do some close, closer-than-close reading, she squeezes washing-up liquid onto the sponge turns off the tap and lifts a bowl, trust the poems to provide everything she needs, excavate a huge pile of rubble from these granite poems, she puts the bowl on the draining board, allow some preliminary sedimentation overnight, then get up and make some bullet points and just type the thing from start to finish, print it off and go cheerfully to her tutorial with the essay rolled up in her hand—

Oh god.

The small brown mug is broken. She went to lift it and something happened, there was a sound and suddenly she is just holding the handle, a brown curl between her fingers, and the handleless brown object is lying in the soapy water.

She wants to make a sound, some sort of low whimper. Instead she picks up the other piece, rinses them both under the tap, and presses the handle back into place, examining the wet join on all sides like Mum would do. No missing fragments: a clean break: yes it can be fixed – but it won't be the same, it will probably never be usable, there will be too much strain on the mended join. What on earth happened. She didn't drop or knock it, the handle just came away in her hand. How long was that faultline instituting itself as she lifted the mug full of liquid, not knowing it was ready to break and flood at any moment. How long did it know before she did.

Rinsing both parts of the mug she lays them side by side on the counter. She looks at them for a moment, sitting there, like a small brown fact. Turns back to the rest of the washing-up.

She brings everything clean and dry back into her room. Puts the crockery down on the shelf and picks up the two pieces of mug again and feels their unnatural separation in her two hands. Actually she feels quite upset. She went out to do a simple task and is returning in disgrace.

She could get Rich to mend it. His gentle doctor's hands wiping the excess glue off the—

No. She will do it. She will set everything out on the desk and plan it all, each motion she will make, where she will put the glue and where she will direct the pressure. Then she will mend it, slowly and carefully. The thought makes her want to cry.

Taking a deep breath she puts the pieces back on the shelf and picks up her phone and turns it on.

A technological pause.

Then silently the screen asserts itself: 3 new messages.

She opens them. One from Mum: is tonight good for a catch-up. One from Rich (of course): is today good to speak about next weekend.

And a long unexpected one from Bridget:

So have u decided about rich yet, is it yea or nay? literally trying to read king lear in bed this does not seem a good plan. nothing will come of nothing zzzzz etc anyway hope ur sonnets r excellent. i was thinking abt coming to your evensong tonite is that ok? xx

Her throat makes a low scrape of discontent. Bridget thinks no to Rich and is offering a couple of blind dates with nice young men from her college. Yesterday she said, because of course she did, Have you got daddy issues or something? As if no one ever thought of that. Even Rich has said it more than once: he does and doesn't like being nearly twice her age, it makes him nervous. But the idea is boring as soon as it arises. The father's absence making him automatically attractive: he was once desired by her mother, now he's gone, and so therefore. She feels how the Freudian story comes crawling after her like a spider, like Shelob giving chase out of the many exits from her lair: psychoanalysis catches her and presses her against the appalling web. Bridget meant it as a joke, but its force is thick as treacle, it oozes and envelops.

~

Last term Bridget had a poem published in *Isis* called 'The Eternal Cow'. Sort of funny and sort of profound were the only set of descriptors Annabel could position correctly when asked for her opinion. It was good, she liked it, it seemed too boisterous, it was pinpoint accurate, it was a little facile. It was (she thinks with work starting to edge above the horizon again) the diametric opposite of the Sonnets. But she must have been especially absorbent when she read it because for a few days it recited itself to her whenever she went out on the meadow: This cow has done badly on its Wordsworth essay, This cow has a crotchety look unbecoming of a creature so well cared for, This cow is one of a gloomy many, This cow bounces my abstract nouns back at me, and so on. It was a longish poem and it highlighted different parts of itself on different days. But it was too loud in her head: in the end she had to banish it entirely.

Anyway Bridget is posh enough that sort of funny and sort of profound is a good territory for her. Yesterday she was cheerful and prickly: Dude I love how you've kept the biggest croissant for yourself. The prickliness is essential in her cheerfulness. She never has the heating on, she sits in a thin jumper full of holes and glows with a hardy unselfconscious pinkness. And she is absolutely not available for romanticisation: she is tall and beautiful and photographs well, but resists all this by often not being very nice, in specific ways not particularly incandescent with holy truth, just small and jabbing. Like starting her complaints with the word *dude*.

Anyway she looks again at the messages. Sends one quick reply, to Mum, and switches the phone off again. Bridget, evensong, Rich, all this she will give attention to later.

∽

She notices a nudge of unhappiness from somewhere else. Ah yes: the brown mug. Sometimes these nudges turn out to be nothing, a wisp from a text, or a hostile memory, and she can locate and dispel it quickly. Not this one. The little brown handle, suddenly alone in her hand. It is upsetting. 'I am upset' she says aloud, calmly. She depended on its hard dark-brownness, its narrowness of shape. On being kept company by it: which makes no sense, she knows this even as she thinks it. But it was an obscure alliance. As if she had decanted some of her own earthen self into the object. Or as if, upon finding the mug, she had found a true flavour of something which she had thought existed only in her imagination, and which one day she would be able to pursue. Now the mug will always have to be left behind, it will have to live out a kind of beautiful retirement on a shelf, never being asked to hold anything.

Anyway she had a plan, didn't she, just before. 'Come on then Annie' she says to herself. Final push.

She sits down, opens the laptop, creates a blank document, finds the centre of the page. Takes up her book and starts to page through. Selects, on a whim, six of the love triangle sonnets – three to the Young Man, three to the Dark Lady – and types them out. Six narrow rooms out of the great big labyrinth. That thou hast her it is not all my griefe. So now I have confest that he is thine. Even just typing them she is stirred, like grass.

She spaces the lines a little more, indents the final couplet of each, zooms out to check each sonnet occupies the centre of its page – then hits Print, leans under the desk to turn the printer on, and brings the cable back up with her to plug into her laptop. A pause: then the electronics catch up with themselves and the printer clacks into action. The pages emerge rapidly one after the other.

And so. She spreads the six pages out on the desk. Six tight poems for her to lick with her mind in a long slow lick right up the spine of each one. Sometimes she thinks, she could be a poet. She has never actually written a poem but that's unimportant, she knows the essence of the poems she would write: small, opaque, complex. About nothing in particular. Producing not so much a meaning as an *effect*. Like a music of words. Well. Perhaps not a coincidence she has never written one.

Or is it, (a new thought,) is it a *poem* she wants to be. A quiet poem on a single page. A small strange one like Emily Dickinson, or an expansive glittering one like the Gawain-poet, or a breathing questing one like Keats. Or even a poem just held in the memory, intact with its commas and colons, not spoken but silent, or just murmured, like rebellious truths are murmured when backs are turned—

No. Detail spoils the clear first thought. She wants to be a poem.

No further delay: with a surge of resolution she addresses herself to her desk and *works*, beginning to climb into each sonnet, limbering herself deliberately inside. Argument, tone. Choice of pronouns. Rhymes. Quatrains and couplet. Extended metaphors, or brief ones just thrown in: or none, or few.

And then more abstractly: how is he representing the gnarl of it to himself. What tensions and torsions are gripping him as he grips his pen. What prejudices. Thou usurer, that put'st forth all to use: a flamboyant double-bind of an insult for a woman who sleeps with his friend not him. Lascivious grace, in whom all ill well shows: you exquisite bundle of lust, you outraging boy. She writes, circles, underlines, lets drop a single exclamation mark onto the page.

At some point the bells at Merton sound all four parts of their sequence, and then chime the hour. One. Two. Silence. She looks over at the two pieces of mug on the shelf: lets a throb of feeling go through: then back down at the desk.

She notices she is also climbing inside something definitive about the Sonnets: that even poems about the same thing, by the same person, next to each other in the same sequence, they are different poems. Each one released into the dignity of its own sheet of paper, they become like six oak trees growing huge in a park, with their own postures and views, their own patches of rot, their own patterns of autumn yellowing. Each needs a consciously refreshed effort of attention.

And, conversely, something definitive about infatuation: how it insists daily that everything is wondrous new, when really it's just the same old tree in the same old soil.

Some while later she heaves her head up, peels her mind off the Sonnets, and finds nearly two hours have gone by. Everything is in shades of white and brown. This civil desk, this excellent room. She has *worked*: here is the proof: a sheaf of poems annotated in her own narrow writing. She has had many small thoughts and written them down, they do not form an argument but there is at least a quantity of them, they have accumulated like seeds. Tomorrow she can mash them up and compress them, and it may not be her best essay ever, but a certain amount of thorough digestion will have taken place.

She gets up, her arms come up above her head in an almighty stretch, lifting her out of her hips. Lamp off, chair under, papers and books to one side of the desk, pens filed back in their pot: this can all be done now with conviction. The feeling of having converted enough of herself to thoughts that qualify. Like an alcoholic in Tennessee Williams she has felt the *click*: something in her has been obscurely satisfied.

Now she stares at the clock, her face tense with calculation, measuring and dividing up. She will not have time for everything. Yoga, yes, she wants to be highly stretched and respectable in her muscles. Meditation, yes, she wants to let the waves crash around in her head and gradually subside. Walking, yes, she wants to walk with a cold blankness, or to think, or else to let the SCHOLAR do both those things on her behalf. Perhaps no evensong then. The exquisite reverences of religion: yes, she can do without all that today. She learned long ago to space herself, that there is no point cramming. The things she does, she does properly.

In anticipation of yoga she is instantly more careful in her movements, stripping swiftly and putting on a vest and her pyjama bottoms, bringing her rolled mat and laying it precisely square on the floor. In one swift push unrolls the whole thing to the end. Steps to the bottom of the mat and stands for a moment.

Then she starts to *shake*: her arms going everywhere – shaking her hands from the wrists like little flapping handkerchiefs – her breasts waggling as she tussles her shoulders back and forth – then holding the back of a chair she shakes each leg in turn from the ankle, from the knee, and then wholly from the hip – then her head wobbling, letting the face-flesh go here and there over the bones – then squats slightly and wobbles the flesh of her bum – and then the same all over again, she stamps from foot to foot and shakes, takes great deep breaths and flings her limbs through space, tries to move *everywhere* inside herself, moving moving moving.

After a few minutes she stops and gets straight down on her back. Lies there, feeling her body. She is warm. A loose vibrant warmth all through her limbs.

She brings her knees up, takes hold of the back of her legs and begins to roll up and down her spine – not entirely smoothly, there is a catch at one or other vertebra – and then with an extra spurt comes up and over onto her hands and knees. Straightaway inhaling and tilting into her hips, all the way through her back shoulders neck, then back the other way arching her body, explaining to Miles how to start the movement at the tailbone and let it travel up—

No: no explaining. She finds her focus again like a small grey circle.

Sinks back onto her haunches and her shoulders come

out into a long stretch, then *up*, her bottom high in the air and a very wholesome force coming down through her shoulders. She pushes into the whole of her palms and fingertips, and settles into stillness. Inhales, then sighs hard through her mouth: something slight goes out of her. A stunning quiet in her mind, which she tries to accept will not last.

Halfway through her sun salutations she realises Rich is her spectator now, she has brought him in to watch her. And has already elaborated some of the detail: how he can't quite appreciate the serious work of her being really *in* her body, working it from the inside out, but he does notice in a professional capacity the way her joints move easily through themselves, as if lubricated. He can admire the steadiness of her plank pose as she lowers to the ground. How she knows which movements to do, in what order. And he likes it when she sticks her bum in the air.

To break his gaze she replaces him with the SCHOLAR, who watches with a different kind of professional interest, perhaps a *truer* interest, whatever that means, but whose upper body strength let's face it would not be sufficient for any of this. She dismisses him with a little smile, and continues.

After several more rounds of raising and bending and lowering and twisting, she turns to the window: to address the trees. Brings her bare foot up to plant the sole on her inside thigh, her knee jutting sideways out. Finds her balance: here. This is her favourite part. There is a deep vertical root going down through her spine and leg into the floor. Then she lifts her closed palms and spreads them joyfully into two overhead branches. She is a tree. She respectfully greets the bare sunlit trees in the bare sunlit winter. She delights in being a tree. The thick sideways branch of her leg threatens to unbalance her, and she squeezes hard and feels the weight of it directing down deep and strong into the ground. What she ought to do here is try closing her eyes, to encourage the ankle to wobble and strengthen itself. But, but, this clear-eyed and open *treeness*. She breathes like a breeze with her face all open in a loose smile, as she never would in front of anyone. After a time, with delicacy and dignity, she removes the leg, places the foot back on the ground, and takes the pose on the other side. She is a tree.

Next she gets down to the ground in a low wide squat like a mushroom, and sits there listening to her hips opening. Wisdom pours through, moving from somewhere to somewhere. She takes a few glad breaths. Then lowers onto her bum and takes a careful roll backwards, letting the momentum lift her legs and back right off the ground, bracing her hands under her ribs, and heaving her legs up to an awkward vertical. She has no great love for the shoulder stand. Her legs so irrelevantly stuck up there, and the flab of her tummy in rolls, staring at her where the vest has fallen away. She breathes with constriction: now she is wholly unlike a tree, no cool summer rain in her leaves and branches, just a hot spike of force down through her, the difficult weight of her body plunging down into her shoulders.

When it feels like too much, she claims the reward: lets her legs tip slowly backwards over her head, her toes approaching the floor from their strange angle, and her whole back is drawn out very deeply. Must keep her neck relaxed or else she will hurt herself. The very deep pull of it: breathes, yes, *good*: then slowly draws in her legs and returns her feet to the mat. How flatly spreading her back now meets the floor, and there are pulses and pinches of energy rushing out through her pelvis. She rolls her head from side to side, feeling the currents surging, and diminishing.

The only thing left is two twists which are utterly benevolent, like two slow fish.

Lying full flat against the floor she can see up through the window: the sunlight in a horizontal slant now, losing its conviction. In the next hour will be a bone-sharp winter sunset. All the trees and walls and rooftops frozen, darkening under the empty sky.

She turns onto her side and gets up slowly. Her body feels good, it feels *used*. Over her strong feet she draws her socks, already softened with today's sweat, and over her head a cotton top and a thick jumper. Then pulls the blue blanket off its chair into her arms and deposits it onto the floor. The glass of water she takes into the bathroom to refill: and the bathroom has such an atmosphere of warmth and water she puts the glass down and sits on the toilet to piss. Empties herself into calmness.

The moving practice, they say, is really only preparation for the sitting practice. Back in the room she pulls the bean-bag cushion into place, gives the whole thing a shake to redistribute the filling, and sits down, her hips and thighs snug and safe against it. She holds down the button on the kitchen timer until it gets to forty-five minutes, and with a *bip* presses start. Pulls the blanket close around her shoulders, in a stately tent over her chest and lap and legs. Her hands in their blue darkness find her knees. She closes her eyes: begins.

The first thing is to notice the wreckage of all the thoughts she has had today. Here they are in a clump, some threatening to become urgent. She tries to see them with a liquid calm interest, not to muscle them out. Here they are. They quail under her gaze, refusing to come in to be gently smiled at, and squirm away.

The bulk, the *lump* of her, resting on the cushion. Her plain white linen mind. She takes some long breaths, feeling her whole torso swell, right down to her pelvis, each of her cells swelling against the next as she breathes in, and then the floor perfect and trustworthy as she breathes out and settles into it. Actually the lumpenness of her body is – the weight of winter is not only metaphorical, her clothes have been feeling tighter – would it not be sweet to be a little leaner, to sit more lightly—

Ah: thinking.

She views the thought with deliberate sympathy, and places it gently down on the ground. This particular group, this gathering gust of thoughts, comes fairly often, the worry about all the sitting she does, wondering how she might lose weight. Perhaps if she did her walk first and then sat down here she would tend less towards this particular—

Ah: thinking, about thinking. Classic.

She is always commenting on her own habits of distraction – no, she catches herself again starting to think. Gazes at it, now a messy gnarl, and with a little exhale sends it down out of her into the floor. Now sits with her mind clarified, with more light in it. A stillness. She can extraordinarily feel her whole body at once, the energy and warmth and breath moving through it, the strength of its engineering, how muscular and supple she is, the opposite of brittle, she cannot just break apart in soapy water—

Ah: thinking. With a kind of panicky sadness.

Tomorrow, yes, she will probably drink out of her other mug with a slightly melancholy sense of the seasons forever turning. And she can enjoy searching for a replacement mug, who knows what unforeseen lovely ceramics she might—

Oh, again. For god's sake. Her hot mind with the sand all churned up.

She tries to let go, properly. She cannot will herself to the good place, it comes from a steady openness, trying to be a hanging sheet in the breeze, heavy under the force of gravity, but allowing ripples to go through. Yes, she is receptive. She is a hanging sheet of thick unbleached canvas. Her breathing comes and goes. Feels the room around her. The immediate yellow comfort, of sitting warm in a room. She steadies her mind on the surfaces of floor and cushion, the places her flesh touches them and does not touch them. She is

JESUS CHRIST what is that she jolts several inches
is it the fire alarm?
the noise stops
AND STARTS AGAIN
oh christ her landline phone that's what it is
the phone that never rings is ringing
and ringing

She is up – shakily, whoa – steadies herself and picks up the phone. 'Hello?'

'Hello you.'

Not a porter, not a student. Rich. Not Oxford: his warm woody voice.

'Oh——hi' she says.

'Ha, don't sound too pleased to hear from me then.'

'Sorry, I——'

Her brain to come back please and fill in this ice-white blankness——she is blind with confusion, should they be speaking on a college line, is it private enough——but they are doing nothing wrong——'I was just meditating.'

'Oh sorry, you do sound a bit spaced out. Do you want me to call back later on?'

'No, I——it's OK.'

Pokes her finger into the tube of the tightly looping cord. Notices the timer on the floor still counting down, thirty-four minutes and twelve seconds, eleven, ten—

He chuckles. 'I don't think I've ever heard you like this before.'

'Yeah, um. Where are you?'

'Oh just at home, you know. Dying to hear from you, your porter very kindly put me through. I did try your mobile but it's been off all day has it?'

'Yeah.'

A little squirming part which might be happy he has called. The rest like huge panes of glass she must try not to smash on him. She notices she has just lied.

'Hey um,' his voice a notch lower, 'what are you wearing?'

'Oh. Pyjamas.'

'What, ha ha, it's nearly four, haven't you gone out yet?'

Could explain that she. But too complicated. 'That's what I'm doing next.'

'OK well pyjama girl, I'm obviously ringing about next weekend, I really do need an answer so I can book a hotel or we'll end up in some grotty B and B.'

'Right.'

'So I just need you to decide yes or no.'

'What———right now?' This is a child's answer.

'Annie it's only two nights, is it that difficult? Or one night even, if you'd prefer. I mean do you want to see me or don't you?'

'Look it's not———I'm just—'

'I know I know. You want to work hard.'

'Yes.'

The timer on thirty-two, thirty-one minutes fifty-nine, eight, seven—

'You know I couldn't sleep last night, I was just imagining what I would do if you were here.'

Helplessly: 'Rich.'

'Do you want to know what I would do?'

Helplessly: '*Rich.*'

'What?'

'I can't, I'm sorry I'm not———I'm too spaced out.'

A sharp exhale. 'OK' he says. 'How about you call me back and let me know before you go to bed. Which'll be about seven p.m. for you, won't it.'

'Yes, OK, um. Sorry I'm just———you know—'

'I get it, it's not a decision-making moment. Anyway I'm on call today so ring the landline if it's before six, leave a message if I'm not there, but I probably will be. Probably fantasising again.'

Another little squirm, but. 'OK' she says.

'Have a productive afternoon.'

'Thanks, you too.'

'Bye.'

'Bye.'

~

He sounded so. Not annoyed, just. She gets into weird states, is how he teased her about it before. If you know the occupant's name and room number the porters do tend to oblige. What was he going to say he would do if she was there.

'Please' she whispers out loud. Still standing by the phone. She takes her hand off it. Her whole body is chill and weak with the shock, the adrenaline, the loud of the phone in the loud of the silence. She didn't tell him about breaking the mug. Or her walk this morning. Or that she saw his message and didn't reply. Isn't it normal for a man to phone his girlfriend. What was he going to say he would do.

Anyway so she has to make the decision today. The afternoon tilts darkly with its new deadline. Better walk now, perhaps, than try to sit through this chemical turbulence. A long-ranging walk, to expand the dilemma into the dusk.

She bends and picks up the kitchen timer, turns it off with a final *bip*, puts it and her cushion back in their places. Goes over to the bed and quickly divests herself of pyjama bottoms and her various jumpers, curving inwards a little as her breasts come bare: his voice is still hanging around, she is having him watch her. With a small headshake she dismisses him. Puts on bra, vest, extra layers, and proper jeans, takes down her dark green jumper from the wardrobe, a second pair of socks, laces up her boots tightly, coat on, scarf, hat. Thus bundled she sits on the toilet and pisses again. In the noise of the flush she rinses her hands, pockets her student card and a ten-pound note and her keys. Picks up her gloves. Out.

~

And so finally, the staircase door falling shut behind her with a click, here she is in the courtyard, in the coldly exhilarating privacy of the evening. She takes an inhale. The smell of the cold stone. A sharp air with the light almost drained out of it.

At the lodge door she braces, hauls open its oaken weight, and holds it for two choirpeople to come in with their gowns over their arms, heading for rehearsal. Then she steps out, and takes the dark lane towards the High Street.

Instantly with her are the SCHOLAR and the SEDUCER: like a dark cloak she puts on. She starts with them walking together, just in a general way, this perpetual walking they do.

First she is the SCHOLAR, hands in pockets, making his slow long strides.

Now she is the SEDUCER, his chin a little raised, smiling faintly, feeling himself possess every inch of space he moves through, gesturing with his gloved hand to something across the street.

She is the SCHOLAR again, with all his attention nailed onto the man next to him, feeling each of those hand gestures as if the hand is passing through his own body.

And now she is the SEDUCER knowing exactly the effect he is having on his friend, and – perhaps because he can see how hard the SCHOLAR is trying to resist – never growing tired of it.

The streets are quiet: with Sunday evening study, with hang-overs, with preparations for worship. Now the SCHOLAR and SEDUCER gain a vividness and evenness, they can fill her whole mind, their mutual fascination can be at full roar. It is interesting – they are both grown men, they are of long acquaintance, yet there is still a flavour of, what – she puts a gloved finger on it lightly as she steps across the street – adolescent glamour. Yes, they have never quite got past this. She starts to shade it in a little. Perhaps they did in fact know each other at school. No: they knew *of* each other. The SEDUCER already bored, lounging in his circle of rich friends: then his interest was stirred one morning by the sight of a younger boy crouching in the icy courtyard, shivering and reading a book with his long limbs sticking out everywhere. Even then, that fierce look of concentration. The SEDUCER enquired, learned his name, watched him a little. She hovers in the SEDUCER's mind, doing the watching. The SCHOLAR looks up and meets her eye: a brief shock.

Yes the SCHOLAR felt himself being watched, was per-plexed. He had no need to make enquiries: for several years he had been hearing reports of this older boy and his exploits, the stories came floating down to him like clumps of weed on water. He began to watch back, and a small habit was established between them, of looks and small smiles and the occasional nod in the corridor. But still they never spoke: their mutual interest shimmered, but never took form. Both felt a tiny puzzlement of loss when the SEDUCER left school. Off he went to London to forge a career, political probably because after all his charm is his originating feature, is deep-rooted and genuine. The SCHOLAR lost sight of him, left school himself a few years later, went off for further study – north into the frozen regions, or perhaps west into the forest, or south into the desert. She considers: she likes the forest best for him. Anyway, point being, they never expected to meet again. It seemed over.

The chip van is parked in its usual spot, with its usual queue of hungover students huddled in coats, arms hugged over their confused stomachs. She thinks of Sanjay and his groaning unfulfilled quest for acceptable food. He has probably recovered his spirits by now and will already be back in the library reading Paine or Hume or J.M. Keynes. His head pushed into his hands, his fingers in his own dark hair: he had no idea he was prickling her interest, he has probably never thought of her that way, she is too shy and strict. What would he have done if she had just stepped over and started to rub his back through his T-shirt, then dipped a hand under the hem and brought it up against his warm skin—

No: enough of that. She spoke to Rich *her actual boyfriend* only ten minutes ago for god's sake. She crosses the street and ducks down the lane by the university church.

At All Souls she goes right up to the gate and wraps her gloved hands around the wrought-iron curls, looking into the quadrangle. This mysterious college: with no under-grads, just a small community of deeply serious Fellows. She peers. No one there. The lawn is lit a sort of black-green by the lamps along the wall. Some scholar could hurry across in a gown, with a hood up even, going to supper or the library, or furtively out to meet a friend. All movements look equally furtive in a darkened quad, especially she imag-ines in All Souls: and she has to imagine it because she's never seen a single person in there. Perhaps this quad is there for show only, to draw the gaze of outsiders, perhaps behind it is a warren of private passageways and rooms, a series of small circular or octagonal courtyards. A rose garden, a knot garden.

Somewhere in the city a bell begins to sound. She continues to peer in. All Souls is the perfect place for the SCHOLAR. She positions his rooms: high up, with a small view, down into a garden and also out through some closely arranged rooftops and buttresses and sprockets and spires. His safe, silent desk, where he accumulates knowledge and loneliness.

Now fuck it's too cold to stand here. With a vengeance of movement she walks.

Faint organ music from inside a chapel somewhere: it stops: plays the same bit: and now there is singing with it. They are rehearsing evensong, all over Oxford they are getting ready to sing, what do they call it, the jewel of the Anglican choral tradition. She is no avid believer but she does like to attend chapel, she likes to watch others get down for the general confession: the dignity of the old kneelers in Fellows' gowns (these men having humbly, beautifully knelt all their lives) and the fervour of the young kneelers in jeans and trainers. And she likes to murmur the words which come easily – having never even tried to learn it she finds the whole text fully formed in her memory – she enjoys hitting each rhythmic beat, tracing the bolts and rivets of Thomas Cranmer's style, the iron-hard wildness of the language, its dark austere glow. Spare thou them O God which confess their faults. Restore thou them that are penitent. O God make clean our hearts within us: one for her, whose heart is very rarely clean within her, look at her lusting after Sanjay just because she saw him in his pyjamas. And there is no health in us. She can recite it all now, walking, including the collects. Lighten our darkness we beseech thee O Lord. And by thy great mercy defend us from all perils and dangers of this night.

A figure coming up the street catches her attention: ah that's because it's Bridget: she noticed her because she already knows her. Here comes that short bob, that look of friendly challenge. A wave, which she returns. And oh god, the message she never replied to.

'Hey hey' Bridget says arriving in front of her, 'so are you not going to evensong then?'

She puts out an arm to receive the hug from the thin, hard body: 'No, I've just realised I didn't get back to you, sorry.'

'Yeah well' Bridget says 'I was sitting there getting annoyed and then I thought well fuck it I'll just set off and if you were there you were there and if you weren't then at least it's evensong and it'll be nice. I'm really hungover anyway so I'm not feeling uber-chatty.'

Evidently there is to be no more discussion of her failure to text back. 'Ha ha oh dear' she says 'what did you do last night?'

'Just a house party at Catriona's but, I don't know for some reason I decided it would be a good idea to have red wine then gin then port then fucking *whisky* for some reason and it all got a bit' – Bridget scrunches up her face – 'just a bit fucking upsetting to be perfectly honest.'

'What happened?'

'Oh mate I just—' There is a tremor in Bridget's voice: and her eyes are shining with wet.

This is utterly unprecedented. She puts out a hand. 'Are you OK?'

'Yeah I just, ha.' Bridget's bare hand comes up, ignoring her outstretched one, and wipes the corner of each eye. 'Yeah I just thought I'd get out for a bit, I'm going to go back soon and make beans on toast get in my PJs and watch like a fucking costume drama or something. God I'm freezing, the old thermoregulation has gone out the window as well, I'm just a wreck of a human being today basically.'

'Well do you want to go and get dinner somewhere, then you won't have to cook?' Can feel her own motives are slightly awry: yes she wants to comfort her friend but also she wants to excavate this further, she wants to know what happened last night, she wants to extract a piece of Bridget's heavily fortified inner life.

'No no honestly' Bridget says 'I'm not even sure I'm up for evensong, I just need the very fucking earliest of nights and a fresh start tomorrow. Have you decided about Rich coming next weekend then?'

'Oh' she says 'no – we're discussing it tonight.' Sounds slightly better than what they both know to be the truth: that she is still putting off the decision which is hers alone to make.

'OK well let me know what you decide won't you.'

'I will.'

'Like make the actual effort to reply to my messages yeah?'

She gives a small smile: feeling tolerated, but only just. 'Yeah I will, sorry. Or we could have a cuppa during the week or something if you want?'

'Oh instead of next Saturday if Rich comes you mean?'

Final attempt: 'Well I meant either way, you know, if you fancied a chat.'

'Oh I mean' – Bridget turns and stares off across the street as if last night is crouching there in a dark corner – 'no look it's fine, you've got your whole routine and to be honest it's really just too fucking messy for words, like it's actually just really boring. Anyway look I am unbelievably cold, I'd better get going.'

'So you're not going to evensong?'

'No I think I will go' Bridget says. 'I could do with a bit of that, you know, bit of God-time. I'd better not be late, see you in due course.'

She stands there watching Bridget walk quickly away. Such clear blue eyes she has and wonderful translucent skin, and then out spill these foul-mouthed little speeches, full of secrecy and show. She sighs and starts to walk again. Could it be an affair of the heart Bridget is beset with. Or did someone give her a drunken dressing-down. She has the brutality of a prophet sometimes, she might easily provoke it. And she has vision of a kind, but she grew up in a big old farmhouse and went to a girls' boarding school in Gloucestershire and seems to have done almost nothing except read books, write poetry, and splash muddily through the countryside on long runs. And go to church: she is a perfect Church of England communicant, utterly *un*communicative about her actual beliefs and adherences but punctiliously devoted to the church calendar. This year she is really going to do Lent properly, she said yesterday with no further explication. Also she is a virgin and won't specify precisely what she has and hasn't done. It is possible she has never been kissed, and possible too that this is why she swears so much.

She turns into Holywell Street. It is nevertheless important to give credit to Bridget, who despite all this (and no doubt because of it) remains very reliable and very interesting. And she does at least metabolise anger quickly, she says she is annoyed and then forgets about it. And last summer she was unexpectedly helpful about the whole Miles and

Katie calamity, she had her over and they went for a long Saturday afternoon walk and came back down the canal and had tea in Blackwell's and browsed the poetry section together. It wasn't anything she said about the actual situation – she more or less limited her commentary to the single word *bummer* – it was more the way she unapologetically fed her own flame: stopping to point out woody nightshade on the riverbank, insisting they stand very still watching a wren until it showed them the location of its nest, raving about some song cycle by Benjamin Britten, explaining the rules of lacrosse with the perfect conviction that Annabel would be interested. Perhaps more obvious sympathy would also have helped, but she managed to flex her mind around to what Bridget was showing her: something about strength of vision, strength of purpose. Like Bridget had her gaze fixed on the sunlit clouds in the distance and was cheerfully ignoring the thunderous loom above her head. Or like, whatever rummaging and fumbling she might be doing with one hand, the other still held its handful of cool grey stones.

Somewhere a bell begins to sound: out of time: with her footsteps. Yes how much more pleasurable to be outside, walking, than to be sitting in a cold chapel. Her legs move her strongly through the streets, her mind begins to move into its favourite realms. She walks, and like tireless wolves her fantasies emerge from the trees and pad alongside her.

So then. The history continues. The SCHOLAR and SEDUCER leave school and go their separate ways. Then fifteen or twenty years later they are introduced at a dinner: meet eyes: and the SCHOLAR gives a soft Ah of recognition.

Yes, the SEDUCER says slowly, I remember you, you were below me at school.

The SCHOLAR nods. Then they begin to talk, and keep talking for the rest of the evening. Each goes home in a slightly different kind of euphoria: fixed in a new fixation. The SEDUCER does what he does best and begins to issue invitations. Evenings of soft talk and strong wine. Each time the SCHOLAR goes to the SEDUCER's country house or his London flat his hopes rise: surely things will – how could this mean anything else? – of course it will happen. He expects any day the grand consummation.

One evening, instead of finishing a paper he has promised a colleague, he dresses carefully and gets on the train to London, thinking perhaps this will be the night. Arrives to his dismay at a large party in full swing. How nice to meet you at last, the SEDUCER's wife says with real warmth. She introduces him to some astonishingly important people, while the SEDUCER gives him a jovial nod from the other side of the room. The SCHOLAR does not dare approach him, not trusting his own powers of composure. He stands making minimal conversation. After a couple of hours he leaves and gets on the train home, sick with disappointment, furious with himself. He finishes the paper very early the next morning and swears, never again.

That was a few years ago now. She pauses as the SCHOLAR might pause, puts a hand on a lamppost in the deserted street, delicately remembering the pain of that evening. Now he is a little more regulated, a little less profligate with his time. He depends, he must remember, on the pleasurable productivity of a life spent largely alone. Until the SEDUCER bloody well puts out – no, she corrects herself, he wouldn't say anything so crass. More like: until something happens that he considers to be life-changing – *paradigm*-changing he might say – she cracks a small smile – until then, he will in no wise change his paradigm, his life.

She reaches St Cross Road, striding easily across the street to the pavement opposite and picking up her pace. Cars come up past her, and something else obtrudes in her mind: herself lying snuggled in the dark with Rich. Burrowing into his body under the eiderdown. All the satisfactions of sex, the internal soreness, the dark murmuring, his little convulsive cry when he comes. His softness and warmth, his hairy encircling pressure, more than any actual features of his body. Richard French sleeping, breathing. Starting to snore. Jerking awake to ask if he was snoring. And always open for business: already hard, or immediately becoming so. He *wants* her. He is too old for her. He is perfect for her.

The time he trailed his hand over her bum on his way to the kitchen sink, and she couldn't help but smile. I see I've found your level, he said. Then he added God I love seeing you smile, it makes me feel like I've really earned it, and he kissed her softly. When we get to summer let's drive to the middle of nowhere and lie by the river all day, yes? She nodded. They kissed, imagining themselves kissing elsewhen, elsewhere.

He is not the first to fix on the smiling thing. It has followed her since school. It is actually true that a girl once came up to Sophy and said You're the only person I've ever seen your sister smile at, she's got a lovely smile, and then just walked off again. And that Miss Francis had read a book one weekend about how in the eighteenth century smiling had begun to be fashionable as an indicator of sensibility and sentiment – with visible teeth, Miss Francis explained, rather than a tight Mona Lisa smile or a beautiful sneer – and then she said, I feel Annabel might have been at home in the pre-smiling era. At which general laughter.

It is impossible, then. Smile, and you lay yourself open to the world. Don't smile, and everyone notices you not smiling. She pulls her coat closer around her, shivering as she walks.

At the park she stops and stands looking through the railings. Dark space. The figures of trees she can just about make out.

In less than four months she will have to bring the whole of her routine and quietness to bear on her Finals. This is what Rich cannot quite comprehend: that she doesn't have time to be infatuated with him. He agrees with her making work a priority right up to the point where he doesn't get to see her: he cannot follow her across the last leap, he cannot enter into the vision of it: where she is fully suspended in her work like a crystal in a glass of water, absolutely silent and solitary.

This is not, admittedly, so much about the exams as about her whole way of being. She wants to compress herself into something small and hard, something dense and complex, like a flint. An opacity that other people might simply bounce off. Or like the roots of a tall tree she wants to be ancient and unquestionable. Wood elves walking softly in Lothlórien: opaque with age, but not old. A huge beech with its smooth grey bark. To be seen without being seen *into*: yes. She wants to stand all day in a deep part of the forest and be perfectly quiet.

It is possible that she, too, is a phenomenologist at best.

She is far out now, beyond the farthest colleges. Her easy stride can cover the city without trouble, Oxford is not large, she can touch its margins and come back again in less than two hours. Her shadow lengthens in front of her, then fades, then reappears behind her, stretching and contracting as she goes through the territory of each lamppost.

Anyway where was she. The SCHOLAR keeping himself strictly secluded in his college. She casts a look up into a passing tree, thinking. What if silence were actually a college policy, in force everywhere except, say, in the porters' lodge and one common parlour, and in the scholars' private bedchambers, where quiet conversation is allowed. At meals either they eat in silence or there is a reading: one of them reads aloud about his research (or *her*? – are there women? – perhaps a few, not many), or else a piece of difficult philosophical or theological poetry, read without hurry. The scholars catch each other's eyes a little, exchange small smiles, maybe thoughtful or inviting faces. Not that they – of course not, all sexual activity would naturally be forbidden within the college walls. But with a little discretion those who wish to can still seek out their preferred adventures. Here the SCHOLAR is a novice. Compared to some of his peers he does nothing, knows nothing. For occasional social fulfilment he goes to another nearby college which has no rules about silence, and his reputation precedes him, they know to expect a superb but singularly inaccessible individual. She feels with pleasure the admiration they have for him. There might be some interesting conversation, followed up in one or two cases by him writing short letters conveying the information the other requested. But he never lets things go any further: perhaps he hardly knows how.

And he accepts – having learned his painful lesson – he limits himself to accepting perhaps one invitation a month from the SEDUCER. This the SEDUCER finds to be a paltry ration. Occasionally, amused and exasperated, he writes to the SCHOLAR, May I instead come and visit you in Oxford? Then no answer comes for over a week, because this too the SCHOLAR has deemed to be politic. And even when he does write back he is non-committal: At present it's difficult to know how my time will be occupied. I have some studies running which it may be impossible to interrupt.

She smiles faintly as she walks. Yes he would be precisely that vague. In fact he is just sitting on a bench in the herb garden making extensive notes on how the plants change and respond to the seasons, from high summer through to deep midwinter and into spring again: a project which could easily relinquish a day or two. It's the calm grey angles of his mind he doesn't want to lose.

This is the system they operate, of unofficial norms and prohibitions. But say – say the SCHOLAR's college holds special dinners a few times a year, at which talking is allowed, and to which the Fellows are encouraged to bring guests. Yes. And there is one such dinner coming up. The SCHOLAR sits very still for an hour and calculates: yes, it is perilous, but he knows his own debt, he is increasingly in danger of losing his only friendship unless he makes himself more available. At the end of the hour he rises, goes to his desk, and carefully writes out the invitation. The SEDUCER writes back the next day to accept it with pleasure.

She stops at the corner and looks down the street, the stretching-away line of dark trees and houses. Now it is the night in question. She is the SCHOLAR waiting at the college gate: arms tightly folded across his thin body, eyes down, going over all the strictures he has put in place for himself. Now the sound of footsteps across the street: his eyes go up: yes, it is the SEDUCER. Her stomach jolts with joy: and she grips a fist of iron control around it. The two men stand and face each other. A low greeting. Now they walk, (she is walking again,) they go across the courtyard, both smiling slightly, each with the other's movement in the corner of his eye. They go into the parlour, where the SEDUCER is introduced to the other scholars. He has exquisite manners, everyone can see it immediately, he is polite and attentive and self-deprecating. Even those who know his reputation and are determined not to be charmed – the SEDUCER gives a full, unfeigned laugh at someone's joke – oh god, they cannot help it, he is magnificent.

They go in to dinner and the SEDUCER asks intelligent questions, directs elegant flirtations at some, makes wry little references back to the SCHOLAR, honouring in front of everyone this unlikely friendship. And the SCHOLAR – well, though not exactly a voyeur he settles contentedly into watching things unfold around him. His colleagues are responding – see, this one has a flush in his cheeks, that one is parting her lips – he watches them develop their own curling questions about what – *that* – would be like. Meanwhile he cradles himself in his own mind. The SEDUCER has made sure of him, and he feels pleasantly made sure of: he can sit suspended in that warmth, he can let it run like a thick river, he can watch others asking the SEDUCER questions he would never ask and he can learn things from the answers. And it is all underwritten by his anticipation of what might happen after dinner, when he will have the SEDUCER to himself: the moment when the two of them will go off together to talk privately, and everyone else, fascinated and envious, will watch them go.

She stops again – likewise suspended, and a little breathless – and looks up at the bare lamplit trees. This is very good. She inhales, and cold air hits the membranes of her nose and floods down her windpipe. Eyes follow the two men out of the room, the SCHOLAR moves with a kind of supreme awareness of the favour he enjoys, he is even a little ostentatious in his movements. Perhaps this will be the night they—

But no: she has a better idea, a more sumptuous drama has presented itself. Say dinner ends. Everyone rises and goes back to the parlour. In a quiet corner, warm with expectation, the SCHOLAR offers his friend a drink in his rooms. And then, oh, the SEDUCER answers:

That's very kind, but I've an early start tomorrow, I think I'll just head back to my guesthouse. Another time.

She exhales slowly through a small round mouth. Yes. It is torment: the SCHOLAR pales: not to have a single private moment with his friend. The SEDUCER has his reasons, he's making a point, that he refuses to wait for weeks and then be expected to be comprehensively available — but he has misjudged the severity of the effect. As the SCHOLAR accompanies his friend back to the college gate he is tight in the throat, he is breaking aground onto sharp rocks. At the gate, a handshake: and the SEDUCER has to pretend not to see the shine in the SCHOLAR's eyes, the deeper colour in the face: the wet and hot that humiliation is. It is so painful because it is so trivial. A grand final rejection would be easier to bear, something accepted as catastrophic, bone-soaking, a flood of the soul. This is much worse: a flick on an exposed humerus.

She walks again, and the SCHOLAR walks too, back to his rooms, his whole body stiff with anguish. One remedy is sharp colourless alcohol in a small glass, many times over. Or else he throws on his warm robes and sets out into the night, to walk the streets of his own misery like a monk walking a labyrinth. Here he is: her long slow paces are his long slow paces. His stillness, even as he walks, not looking around him, just letting his gaze sink into the shadows. He will walk like this for hours.

She leaves him there and now she is the SEDUCER, also walking, on the way back to his guesthouse. He is walking fast — yes because he has a destination, but also because he is a little agitated, a little annoyed with himself. His nose is cut off and his face is properly spited. Just for the sake of that small triumph: how petty of him, how contempt-ible. As he walks he is mentally composing a note, asking the SCHOLAR to join him at an eating-house for an early breakfast. Something feels good in the idea of meeting for breakfast – a quiet, rare intimacy – but does he dare ask? The SCHOLAR will be working, he always works in the mornings. They could send refusals back and forth like this for days.

But very quickly: the SEDUCER returns to his guesthouse, scrawls the note, gives it to the message boy (they live in an unspecified pre-telephonic era), the boy runs to the college and gives it to the porter, the porter takes it up to the SCHOLAR's room, the SCHOLAR opens the note, lifts a finger to ask the porter to wait, strides over to his desk, takes a pencil and writes the single word *Yes* at the bottom of the note, folds it shut and reseals it, gives it back to the porter and shuts the door, his heart beating with the suddenness of reversal and decision-making. The boy runs back with it to the guesthouse. The SEDUCER has his answer in less than half an hour. Now they both can and can't sleep.

Or alternatively – as she spots a gap between cars and strides across the road – alternatively the SEDUCER changes his mind about going straight home. It has been an unsatisfactory evening, he also wants to walk for a while. His body will ease, perhaps, the mistakes his mind has made.

And so, this is the point, she can have the two of them meeting coming opposite ways down a deserted street. Each recognises the other's unhappiness: this then is the truth of the matter. They hesitate, then come to meet, smiling.

She stops by a bare stone wall. Places them, standing a few feet apart, and one of them – this feels like a SCHOLAR line – he murmurs, Shall we have a drink then?

She breathes out the words very softly, enjoying how both of them are possessed by relief, deep in a gulf of affection. Anyway they turn, they are back in their pinnacle position: walking side by side. She reaches the corner and turns left onto the main road, towards home.

Even with the cars and flashing cyclists and a bus steaming up the road past her, there is a true quiet between all the sounds, a Sunday evening quiet. A couple comes towards her carrying shopping bags, talking and laughing. The woman takes one smiling glance at her, without interest.

Every so often she attempts scenes of actual intimacy between the SCHOLAR and SEDUCER. They deserve each other, after such lengthy toil, after all the nonsense with the COLLEAGUE, all the toying and teasing and tolerating, they ought to reach the full scope of each other. And she wants the pleasure too, of lifting the sluice and letting all that tension pour through, into gorgeous expression: the unspeakable, flooding into the ecstatic.

For instance, a scene where late at night the SEDUCER begins to talk: admits, finally, what he has been feeling. The SCHOLAR is sitting up in bed, listening with his eyes half closed, doing a very good job of keeping still. The speech ends: they look at each other: finally it is said. Then the SCHOLAR says, Come here. The SEDUCER bristles, he takes orders from no one, a man in his position, there is no way – the SCHOLAR is waiting with a cool hard look – and the SEDUCER finds himself getting up and crossing the room, and that is that.

Another: the SCHOLAR, very ill in bed, waking briefly and murmuring. The SEDUCER leans over him, reassures him, puts a single soft kiss on his lips even as he lapses back into sleep.

Another: the SEDUCER and the SCHOLAR are visited by a journalist who has managed to photograph them in an alley. He shows them the pictures. The SEDUCER is gasping, then his face is tipped back against the wall, then he is clutching the dark head. Actually the SCHOLAR is only identifiable in the final two photographs, as he gets up and examines the knees of his trousers for stains, while the SEDUCER leans heavily back and smiles and rubs his eyes. Now looking at them the SCHOLAR is speechless with terror, the shame of exposure, his probable expulsion from the university. The SEDUCER is more worldly: he delivers a series of perfectly judged threats while maintaining a mien of cheerful indifference to the content of the photographs. The journalist leaves thoroughly chastened, the SCHOLAR slumps in relief, the SEDUCER looks again at the photographs and smiling puts them into his desk drawer with a wry remark: How kind of him to record that evening for posterity.

Another: the SCHOLAR arrives at the SEDUCER's house very early in the morning. They stand in the hallway, they glimmer with anticipation. In the afternoon they rise from bed and eat a late lunch with the autumn sunlight slanting in. The SEDUCER peels an apple with a thin silver knife.

More bicycles come past her up Turl Street, some with proper lights, others just dark rattling shapes. She is still swollen with fantasy, but noticing also the common feature of all these scenes: that she has never successfully got the SCHOLAR and SEDUCER to kiss or fuck at length in front of her. As if they suspect her intentions no longer to be honourable they won't do it, their dignity exceeds hers. Like they both know, and she knows really, that since they are both men it has nothing to do with her. That however two men may treat with each other she should stay well out of it.

Or – is it that they are both *her*. They have both sprung from her mind, and therefore perhaps it has everything to do with her. She comes cold into this new line of thought. Yes perhaps it would be too much like having herself fuck herself. Every touch, lick, thrust is hers and hers again, hers twice over, enacted by one and received by the other. And should not that be exciting? synchronous? a redoubling of pleasure, and beautifully perfectible? – but it isn't. The SEDUCER pushes his thumb with satisfaction into the SCHOLAR's mouth, the SCHOLAR moans and tips his head back in ecstasy – yes, it gives a flash of brilliance, but it is immediately cut off. Somewhere she is prohibited from a full, final consummation.

She reaches the High Street again. An ambulance is flashing past, no siren. She waits for it, then steps across the street in its wake, watching it overtake a bus and head off east towards the hospital.

Where was she. Yes, sometimes it's as if the SCHOLAR and SEDUCER work together to lock her out, to bar her from comprehensiveness. Their actual faces, their actual voices, their specific excitabilities, even their *names* for goodness' sake, she doesn't know any of it. She can fix details: that the SCHOLAR's genitals dangle almost comically from his thin pelvis, that the SEDUCER's buttocks have a nice solid curve to them, that the SCHOLAR's pleasure is intensely anal and he feels his orgasms rip through him right from the rectum. That the SEDUCER is, perhaps, waiting for someone to take control of him at last, to reduce him to a quivering mass of arousal and relief. She has these vivid undeveloped notions, these micro-theories, yes, but she cannot get to the essence of them. Almost as if they were real people. Almost as if they weren't real people.

An image comes to her: a cat's cradle. A set of threads held tight – a pause – then one man reaches in and inserts his fingers, takes hold of crossed threads, and pulls them round into a new space of ambiguity and anticipation. The other examines the new pattern and smiles, seeing what has been done, devising a response. They pass the looped string back and forth, apparently having started this game without considering that a cat's cradle has no end, it has no triumphant final position but just goes round and round the same four or five patterns. The unpleasantness of letting the string slacken and slither off their hands, that is the alternative, that is what would happen if they let each other go, or equally if they fell into each other's arms for ever and ever. Either way, they would no longer need her. Their shimmering chaste fixation – her shimmering chaste fixation – would be over.

And as she nears the college gate, another thought: is not the cat's cradle the very image of the Sonnets? A single loop of string arranged and rearranged, crisscrossing over itself in self-references, self-shaping. The poet with his four hands. And her, likewise a fantasist, with hers.

Coming back into college she confirms, yes, the chapel windows are lit, the door is closed, evensong is well under way. She should go straight to dinner. But she finds herself doing something unscheduled: heading away from the dining hall, past the chapel, across a cold quadrangle and into a narrow passage. At the end of the passage she stands and looks out into the garden, thinking.

The dark lawn stretches away towards the flowerbeds. The two huge bare trees proclaim their knowledge of the night. This is her favourite place in the college, here in the archway: a place from which to see the garden, to regard it, to step into it. It is her place. She came here aged what, sixteen – nearly four years ago now – one of a group of anxious sixth-formers, her head a blur of colleges and prospectuses. There was a downpour and everyone crowded inside. For some reason she separated herself from the group, found her way to this passage and stood in the archway, shoulder against the stone wall, watching the dull summer rain on the dull summer greenery, thinking about this thing called Oxford.

And on the train home (she remembers suddenly) she formulated a scene: the SEDUCER finding her there alone watching the rain. Talking softly in her ear, putting a hand on her shoulder to turn her towards him and slowly kissing her, pressing her against the wall right there (right *here*) in the passage. She turned and twisted on the rough seat, lulled by the movement of the train, sleepily maddened by the fantasy. Oh it was simpler then. The SEDUCER was more interested in women. She herself was both more and less interested in men.

She ought to get to dinner, the canteen will close. She continues to stand there, inhabited by a dense foliage of thought.

The SEDUCER is really a benevolent kind of person: there is a straight path from his desires to his satisfactions, he likes a cup of hot tea after a cold walk, and he always needs the SCHOLAR eventually. In various hollows and compartments of her mind are other figures, characters from children's books and Disney films – the Demon Headmaster, who coolly removes his glasses to hypnotise pale, clever Dinah – the cartoon Frollo, infatuated with the gypsy girl Esmeralda and desperate to burn her at the stake – and even, in her more shivery moments, the chilling, volatile, murderous Bill Sikes. She is underwritten by this: this catacomb of her own bleak, confusing desires.

One chamber is actually inhabited by a real person, whom she keeps there as proof that reality can, just occasionally, meet her darker requirements. His name is Professor James Sligo. She only met him once, last year, but he did enough. He sat at their table eating their roast beef and drinking their wine and there was something about him, a smooth sliding kind of energy, of which he however kept so much back, moving slowly to serve himself horse-radish sauce, his gaze moving to whoever was speaking, his mind like a great mass of warm water in the room. She was prickling – fretting – jittery with – she didn't understand what was happening. She was giving him coy looks without even deciding to: and every time she did he gave a kind of gleam, he made a transfer of energy across the table and she felt it enter her like knowledge. Then when Mum was turned away talking to the others he turned his full gaze on her and gave her a *look*, and her stomach began to weaken and rot. It was real, he was on to her. She said less and less: starting to shiver with excitement, worried she might disqualify herself by saying something pretentious or irritating. Though maybe that was what he liked, maybe her adolescent stickiness juxtaposed well with – whatever he was imagining. Which was not entirely clear. It wasn't exactly that he would manoeuvre her into position and fuck her until she was bruised. That thought was there, he was *backed up* by it, but it was not exactly that. She sat there thinking desperately, trembling whenever his eyes swept across her eyes. It was more like – if they could achieve a moment when they were both thinking the same thing – perhaps imagining his firm grip on her flanks as he fucked her – a moment where he could look at her and be sure, and she could look at him and feel transparent in a single white line—

She takes a long slow inhale of cold air. The organ has started in the chapel and they are singing the Magnificat, the joyful song of Mary. For he hath regarded the lowliness of his handmaiden. Outside the chapel, inside her body, her chest stomach cunt are all starting to ache with longing.

Anyway it didn't happen. She was dispatched to the kitchen to make coffee and when she came back they had moved to the sitting room and his gaze had moved off, like a slow shark losing interest. One brief moment when she took his coffee over to him and poured the milk into it and murmured Say when, he looked up to meet her eyes and the same thing thumped inside her, the milk jug shook slightly in her hand. But then she had to go and sit down on the other side of the room and his attention returned to her mother, her sisters. She curled her legs up to show him her snug denim thighs, but no. After half an hour he stood up to leave, he kissed Mum's cheek and shook hands with all three girls, the door closed, his car slid off down the gravel. The house sprang back: a house full of women. Annie love, did you not like him, you hardly said a word.

She sat up half that night wide-eyed and inflamed, curled in her pyjamas, plunging the evening again and again into her tank of analysis. Who was this man. How had he known how to work her. She looked up his page on the university website as if it would contain clues, which it didn't. She went reluctantly to bed and lay there staring into the darkness. For a few days she was transfixed with waiting. Of course he would not be satisfied, of course he would contact her to arrange things. With total certainty she expected something in her Oxford email. All he needed was a good guess based on her first name, surname, college. But later she realised he would have to know her surname was Percy not Campbell: and reluctantly she concluded he probably wouldn't know that. Anyway nothing ever came, and although when she got back to Oxford she seized her post out of her pigeonhole in the hope that he had – but no, there was nothing. Gradually her mind loosened its grip: it wouldn't happen, it was over. The episode was for reference only. In the end she stripped a few things from it and fed them into the SEDUCER. The sense of his gleam, his *glitter*, she tried to clarify to herself what it described. A slight swell in his shoulders as he had held her gaze. A tightening of the muscles around his eyes, and a restrained kind of pleasure around his mouth. His absolute accuracy playing this absolutely specialised game.

And then – she counts them off on her mind's fingers, the SEDUCER, James Sligo, and then – lurking, always lurking, is the man who lives in the woods: the green man. He is the worst, and also the best. He has no interest in whatever sexuality is supposed to be, he is neither seductive nor affectionate, just full of curling, fleshly knowledge. He lives secretly, cannily, on land he does not own. And he is – strange. There is something about him that even when you look him full in the face you can't see what he looks like. He's sort of grey you would start to say, then your tongue would go heavy and you'd be stumped for anything more to describe. Indeed his interest is with the mouth. He makes his own exquisite implements. A white china doorknob he found and fixed to a buckled strap. The strap goes around her head, the cold doorknob into her mouth. Also a cage for the tongue: he likes to push his own tongue in and feel her squashed and straining behind the thin twiggy bars of the cage. Also a gag which can be stuffed with herbs before being fitted. Her full mouth, a fragrant speechlessness. He surveys her: I like to see you munching on my herbs. This line took her surging over the edge and drained her so completely she couldn't move for fifteen minutes afterwards. The whole thing had come to her fully formed. Bravo, mind.

She stands very still, trying not to shiver. The green man turns, smiling, and shows her: the mucky unvisited forest clearing. The half-light. And the black pond: its surface covered in scum, with no movement of water, no known depth. She swallows and takes a step towards it. The green man puts a hand lightly on the back of her neck, urging her on.

The pond has waited for her for years. Somehow this is where it all comes from – everything – all. Even with their fierce glamour the SCHOLAR and SEDUCER are no more than a breeze blown across the surface of that black water and off into the world: yes, she can look back out of the woods and see the two of them strolling in bright sunlight. The real thick stuff comes from in here, from under the water. It generates scrolls of arousal – huge oaken arches of desire – yards of crazed embroidery. It waits for her: not to fall into it by accident, but to step willingly into the shallows, and *ultimately*, (the word holds everything,) to submerge herself with shuddering ecstasy, not expecting to come back up.

Now there is a whole thick rope of longing in her. It pulls up through her cunt, her belly, her chest, her throat, her straining mind. She *wants*.

Or maybe it's the cold penetrating too deep. Perils and dangers of this night: yes indeed. She turns back, and goes to dinner.

In the bright loud warmth of the servery she is met by Jan's smiling eyes and flushed face. 'Hello love' Jan says 'what would you like?'

'More peas' shouts a guy in the kitchen, hauling a vat of peas onto the counter behind Jan.

She can feel the warmth coming off it all. Taking a tray she asks for lamb and potatoes and gravy and peas and green beans. The simple Sunday colours of green and brown and yellow pile onto the white college plate, covering its small blue crest.

'Any pud?'

Eyeing the bowls of apple crumble and custard, which god look delicious, 'No thanks' she says.

'That crumble's a new recipe Helen got from her course, are you sure you don't want any?' Jan pushes a bowl towards her and they meet eyes again. Hard not to return the smile.

'Oh OK thank you' she says and takes the crumble. After all she did walk an extra hour today. 'How are you?'

'Oh fine, just as usual you know' Jan says moving along to the till. 'Looking forward to getting home and reading my book by the fire. That's four twenty when you're ready love. How about you, are you doing OK?'

She nods. 'Not bad.' Suddenly shy for anything else to say. Fishing her student card out of her coat pocket she presses it on the terminal, smiles her shy version of a smile, and that's it. As she gets cutlery, napkin, water glass, and carries her tray out of the servery, her face is all hot. For god's sake she could have asked Jan about her book, or about the crumble. Too embarrassed to chat, because Jan is so nice to her.

~

She reaches the doorway into hall – assumes an expression of some kind, her chin up – and goes in. The bright rows of table lamps, the mess of colours and clothing and voices. A few heads turn – the socially vigilant members of college – but thankfully in the corner is Ciara, and two other heads which must be Miles and Katie. More eyes notice and then stop noticing her as she goes over.

Ciara sees her first and smiles, 'Hey Annabel,' and Miles and Katie turn in unison, and a general shuffle makes room for her to climb around the end of the table and put her tray down next to Ciara's and take her coat off and fold it neatly beside her, and finally sit down.

All this done, sitting in her dark green jumper surrounded by people, she allows herself a single glance at Miles: but he is already looking at her. 'How are things?' he says.

'Yes OK' she says. Unusual to see him: she never expects him in hall any more, nor Katie neither. Tilting the heavy jug over her water glass she draws up her whole day in her head, hot and cold and walking and sitting and thinking and reading and speaking on the phone. Nothing offers immediate material. She lowers the jug back onto the table and says 'Just trying to do my Sonnets essay.'

'Oh yeah me too' Ciara says, and then grins, 'it's going weirdly well actually, I'm going back to the library after this to literally *finish* my essay, impressive huh?'

'What are you writing about?' Miles asks Ciara: calmly, as if out of pure professional interest, as if he does not also have a fast-approaching deadline, as if he has no skin in this game.

'Gender' Ciara says, 'so I'm considering how the language changes from the Young Man to the Dark Lady sections, and thinking whether there are any exceptions, like moments where he speaks to the man more like how he speaks to the woman, and vice versa. How about everyone else?' Ciara looks at her, then at Miles, and Katie's head turns too: and suddenly they are all looking at Miles.

'Well' he says, he presses a fingertip on his fork handle and draws it to lie exactly parallel to his knife, 'something about self-reflexivity I think, or maybe performativity, so, why does the speaker break his silence every time, for each sonnet. If the alternative to each sonnet could be silence. What is the compulsion to speak.'

He looks at her: for a moment they register, that he has put an *idea* into the air. She looks down and brings a piece of lamb to her mouth.

Katie says 'We looked at sonnet sequences last term for the Renaissance paper, I couldn't believe how many there are, I read something like, there were three hundred *thousand* sonnets published during that period.'

The lamb is, well, she will be working on it for a while yet.

'Just in England' Miles says 'or across Europe?' Again as if he is merely a professional asking another professional: and he seems to realise it: he takes hold of (presumably) Katie's hand under the table and moves an inch closer.

'Yeah good question' Katie says, 'I can't remember,' she is smiling at him, she doesn't care any more about sonnets.

She adds a few bits of potato and green beans into her mouth: the lamb can continue as a background project.

Tries, for a second, to look dispassionately at Katie. She is very clever, certainly. But more like a schoolgirl is clever: a kind of eager rapidity in her cleverness. Like, she is a *student*, not a scholar who sits with a text rolling it around in her head. She will get her English degree like ticking it off a list, and move on to something else.

At the door the first choirpeople start to come in from evensong, some still wearing their gowns. Finally her throat gets hold of the whole lot of vegetables and potato and lamb, and swallows it.

'Annabel what are you writing about?' Miles says.

'Um.' She smiles down at her plate to prepare for embarrassment. 'Good question, I haven't actually—'

'Hey pals' comes a voice. They all look up, and the voice is tall Emma Weeting, lowering a tray onto the corner of the table. There is more heaving and shuffling of trays and she sits down heavily next to Katie, 'God I totally lost track of the time I thought I was going to miss dinner. So English gang, this is nice, what's the biz?'

'We were just waiting on tenterhooks to hear what Annabel's Sonnets essay will be about' Miles says. He is so dry he doesn't even smile.

'Oh christ' Emma says, 'this whole Shakespeare paper when will it be *over*. Anyway,' her voice goes quieter, a bit grim, 'has everyone heard about Grace?'

'Grace who, Cornish?' Ciara says.

'Yeah, so maybe like an hour ago they had to get the paramedics to her room?'

She looks up.

'Shit why?' Ciara says.

'So she has the room opposite mine' Emma says, 'next to Annabel's, anyway I heard Chris the porter knocking on her door and shouting Grace are you there we're worried about you, and I went and poked my head out and they were like Grace we're coming in OK, and Chris and Geoff went into her room and I think she must have been unconscious, they kept saying her name like they were trying to wake her up, and then Chris said I'll call an ambulance you call her parents, and Geoff came out and asked me like, who are her friends around college is there someone who could come in the ambulance with her, so I was like I have absolutely no idea she's not exactly a socialiser, I actually knocked on your door Annabel and you weren't there right?' – she shakes her head – 'and anyway he said her parents hadn't heard from her for a few days so they called the college and said could they check on her, apparently Christmas wasn't great she had a bit of a wobble et cetera. So yeah eventually the ambulance came and they had to stretcher her down, I think Chris went in the ambulance, and now she's in hospital. Fucking horrendous,' and she puts a potato in her mouth.

'Jesus' Ciara says.

'I know' says Emma through her potato.

This is undeniably major. And yes, grim. She surveys Emma: trying to gauge her enjoyment telling this story. But no, an absolutely straight and solemn face. She pushes her own fork into her own potato, with no specific intention of eating it. Tries to remember what day she last saw Grace, when she last heard definite movement next door. So all this morning while she was working—

'Oh my god' someone says further along the table, 'don't say it's going to snow, I bloody hate snow,' and some noises of disbelief and laughter.

She looks up at Miles: his eyes meet hers briefly and then look away. He told her once that he – how did he say it, she can't remember, something about stomach problems as a child and the consequent anxiety – anyway it explained his thinness: as not entirely native.

'So' Katie says, 'what, she just collapsed?'

Miles turns to her. 'She has anorexia.'

Katie's hand comes up over her mouth and he makes a comforting little smile. All these boyfriend gestures he has evolved. 'Yeah' he says. 'But it's long term, isn't it, I think she's had it since before she left school?' He is asking her, Annabel.

'Yeah you hung out with her a bit last year didn't you?' says Ciara. Also asking her.

'Well' she says. How to be truthful and delicate. 'Not last year. First year we did a bit. But yeah she was ill already, maybe not *as* ill, but.'

She shrugs and the others nod. Grace was very funny and always made interesting suggestions for outings, but – she just *talked* too much. They tried running around the meadow together and Grace talked every single stride, and all three times she herself came back wanting to put her head in a bucket of cold water. Likewise in the Ashmolean Grace compulsively monologued the whole exhibition of German drawings, every flicker of an idea into rapid sentences, jumping from Wow that's amazing how do you think they knew when to stop making marks to Oh Venetian blue paper is so beautiful I'm going to look it up when we get back to college to Not sure I can en-Dürer any more of this, get it, ha ha let's get a coffee. She found Grace annoying, and a bit alarming, especially her tiny wrists, her thick tights.

Suddenly she remembers the ambulance going down the High Street.

'I had a friend at school with an eating disorder' Ciara says 'and it was really tricky actually, like I loved her so much, but she started to lie quite a lot and she was often in a bad mood and she could be so bitchy, and my dad said to me in the end, because we were like fifteen, he said yes she's ill and it's very sad but you don't actually have to be friends with someone if they behave like that.'

She says 'Grace wasn't – she was never bitchy or anything, we just, it was just.'

She shrugs and stops talking. Grace never ate in front of her. And almost never acknowledged she was unwell: the one allusion she did make was about not having periods – Because of all my eating stuff she said, and honestly it's pretty awesome, no tampons no towels nothing! Anyway are you going to watch the rowing on Saturday – and that was it, the hatch was barely open before it snapped shut. It was a closely guarded, wide open secret.

Miles is looking at her. His face is so extremely still: he could be thinking major contempt, or recalling what she said to him about Grace back in the summer. Or he could be wondering, will this throw a greenish light on my own food issues.

'There was a girl at my school who *faked* an eating disorder' Emma says, 'she used to make this massive thing of going to the bathroom straight after lunch and made so much fuss about finishing her food and we would all sit there with her trying to like *coax* her into eating. And then other days she was just totally fine you know? In the end we were like look Jules, the world has enough shit in it without this fucking *pantomime*.' As Emma speaks she is rapidly cutting up and eating her vegetarian sausages and potatoes and banishing an overcooked one to the edge of her plate, her cutlery turning and flashing against the food.

With relief she herself puts one last bite of lamb into her

mouth and concludes matters on her own plate. Takes up her spoon to pierce the skin of the crumble and custard.

'But what' Ciara says, 'so she definitely didn't have an eating disorder?'

'Nah' Emma says, 'I mean it was like some days she remembered she was meant to have it and then other days – because Grace doesn't come to meals does she, like I literally don't think I've ever seen her in here. Whereas this girl Jules always came to lunch and sometimes she ate totally fine, but then other times it was like she wanted to be *seen* refusing to eat, you know?'

The crumble is hot and cinnamony and extremely good.

'But don't you think' Katie says suddenly, and then stops.

Emma stops her cutlery and looks at Katie. 'What?'

Not a *what* it seems safe to reply to. Emma has been known, after a twenty-minute debate in tutorials, to end with Well I still think, and then to complain later that nobody tried to see her point of view.

But Katie is weighing up her own thoughts: and, more prepared, speaks again. 'I guess I was just wondering what would make someone pretend they had an eating disorder.'

Emma makes a scrunch with her face: it's scornfully obvious: 'She was just an attention-seeker basically.'

'Yes' Katie says 'but – why would someone feel they had to get attention that way, is what I'm getting at.' Her voice has gone calmer, quieter: someone, a parent presumably, has taught her well: this is how to disagree with people.

'God knows' Emma says, 'maybe her parents didn't like *nurture* her enough or something. I don't really care, it doesn't mean you have to lie.'

Katie gives up: she sees her subside and turn to Miles. '*West Wing*?' he says and she nods and they both start extracting themselves from the benches, pick up their trays, and Miles says a general 'See you soon,' and they go. Emma swings herself round the table to fill the empty space, and carries on eating as if nothing has changed.

'They are so cute' Ciara says.

'I know' she says: reluctantly meaning it. Katie is more endowed with – it sounds bad but here it is – more endowed with *personality* than she realised. They are a good couple. They tend to sleep out in Katie's shared flat with a proper kitchen, Miles likes to cook. Tonight they will go back to his room and curl up in bed and watch their TV show on his laptop. And then tomorrow go to a cafe and have a sweet little Monday morning breakfast and talk very quietly. They are like—

'How are you anyway Annabel' Ciara says, 'did you say you haven't chosen what to write about for the Sonnets? Do I sense an essay crisis looming?'

'Ha' she says. 'Well. Maybe a bit.' She feels the lump of herself not wanting to speak. Pushes herself on: 'Sometimes I really wish he would set us essay questions. Or even just a general theme, like, write about imagery, write about form, or.' She stops and resets. 'I just find the Sonnets kind of – slippery.'

'Mmm yeah I know what you mean' Ciara says, 'I do find like, you can't say anything about them that they haven't already said a million times better.'

'I – yes' – Looks at Ciara. Tries to formulate a reply.

'Maybe that's not what you meant though' Ciara says, smiling from under her mass of dark curly hair.

If the SCHOLAR reminded himself to behave well he would say, and this is what she does in fact say: 'No actually that's, that's exactly what I meant.'

Ciara makes a little noise in the back of her throat: thoughtful, or surprised maybe, or satisfied. Then she says 'Do you want to go to the Bear and get a half or something? I need to finish my essay but if we make it a quick one.'

'Oh' – she catches herself about to automatically say no, and shoots back at herself, it's only half a pint for god's sake – starts to say 'Yeah maybe' – then remembers – 'oh no I can't, I need to call my boyfriend.'

'Ooh boyfriend' Emma says loudly, then stops. Evidently can't let this news pass without comment: but cannot quite get up the momentum for an interrogation.

'OK' Ciara says, 'another time maybe.' Smiling again, 'That means I have to actually go and write my bloody essay now doesn't it.'

They all get up together and take their trays over, and Emma banters a bit with Paolo as he sorts the dirty crockery into racks, she is one of those people who knows every member of college staff by name and they all like her. Then together they go out of hall and along the stone corridor. The familiar fist, the faecal fist, is starting to grow in her pelvis.

Ciara forces the heavy latch up and heaves the door, and they step out into the freezing quad. A cold smell: and the faint trace of cigarette smoke. 'See you' Ciara and Emma say and she says 'Bye.' As she walks off she hears Emma behind her say 'I'd be up for a quick half if you want,' and Ciara saying 'Nah, I'm just trying to procrastinate, I really should' et cetera et cetera. 'Fair enough' Emma says. When she glances back she sees Emma's tall form going off, alone, towards the common room.

She heads for her own corner of the quad: refuses to

glance up at Miles's lit window. For a moment the dark flavour of her walk, the SCHOLAR and SEDUCER, the garden, the black pond. But also the fresh stir of Ciara's invitation: which was, possibly, just for her. She does like Ciara. She's cut in the same smart lively funny mould as so many Oxford girls, or rather she has assimilated herself into the genre – she is Oxford-lively, and Oxford-funny, and Oxford-smart, she can sprawl in the common room with a takeaway cappuccino being wry about Chaucer – but she is also *nice*: quite possibly *genuinely nice*. The words take on the italics of surprise. Maybe after their tutorials tomorrow they could – she starts to compose a message in her head—

No. She has a boyfriend to decide about first. Finish what's on your plate.

Going back upstairs she gets a sudden flavour of her own body. The way she is cut and arranged. Neither big nor small nor tall nor short. No particular bulges or bones. *Neat* might be one word. And functional: which her bowels are extremely keen to prove: this is a strong one, starting to grind like a stone. God she has to – she puts a spurt on, half running past Emma's door, Grace's door, her key in her hand. A glance back at Grace's white door.

Another seizing of her insides and she unlocks her own door charges into the room throws her coat to one side lurches into the bathroom shuts the bathroom door and pulls her jeans down.

And oh *god*, all the forces combine in her lower belly and it comes out like a snake all stinking and slippery and hits the water with a *plump*. Christ what do they put in that food. There is more – her body produces more force and more comes out – her whole lower half working and pushing – she is that phrase *bearing down* on it – and it goes on and on, another splash and another, her muscles gasping and pulsing again, pushing to clear every last morsel.

Finally it subsides: she sits there, arms braced across her knees, her head down. Behind her is a heap of shit in the toilet, half in half out of the water to judge by the smell. Slowly she moves, glances back at the brown mess, and begins the tedious process of wiping herself, the repetition of smaller and smaller smears on white paper. Then gets up, shuts the lid on the whole lot and flushes. Covers her hands in water and college soap and thoroughly cleans them and dries them on her towel. That was eventful. Not for the first time she wonders if everyone gets this after hall food, do shits come slipping out of them like small whales, is there all over college a sudden roar and rush of water as they are flushed away.

Anyway now she has to call Rich. She is lighter down there, also a little dry in the mouth. Perhaps this will help, or. 'Christ Annabel' she says aloud. What is she going to do.

Mum has been sending live updates. 17:13: Of course eight-ish is fine to speak, we'll call you then. 18:51: Bit of a change of plan darling, Granny isn't feeling well so I'm going to go over, maybe ring Caro and Sophy and you and I can try and speak later this week? 18:53: Just text Sophy and let her know, she's in charge tonight!

She deletes the messages and returns to the home screen: the time, 19:12, suspended over a photo of the five of them, Granny smiling among her daughter and granddaughters, at Christmas. No more delays: Rich. 'Right hold on a second' she says aloud. Sits down on the bed, lays the phone down next to her. There are what, three choices. Say yes plain and simple to next weekend. Or put him off but with the assurance she'll see him lots at Easter, maybe they'll even tell Mum, she *does* want him, honestly she does. Or a definite, general, final No.

Something occurs and she smiles faintly: she is both Bassanio and Portia: hoping very much to choose the correct casket, but the caskets are also hers, or rather they are *her*, and also she has no idea, still no bloody idea, which one to choose.

Almost without deciding she lifts her phone and calls Rich.

Shit it's ringing. Why is she playing this game of brinkmanship with herself—

—and then his voice, 'Ah-ha, it's pyjama girl, or am I out of date now?'

Different responses struggling several ways in her head, but she says 'Yeah I am actually dressed now.'

'Oh excellent, have you had dinner?'

'Yeah I went for a walk and then came back and ate in hall,' and then came up here and emptied my entire

182

alimentary canal for some reason, but she doesn't say this.

'Wow, you mean you pretended to be a normal sociable human being for a bit?'

'Er yeah I suppose so' she says. What is she going to say about next weekend, he will ask her any moment.

'Sorry' his voice says suddenly. 'Jesus sorry, that wasn't a very nice thing to say.'

'Oh.' She replays what he said, registers his meaning. 'It's OK.'

'OK. Sorry. Well anyway how was dinner?'

'It was fine. Ciara who does English with me invited me for a drink.'

'Oh, you should go, go out and have a nice time.'

'It's all right, I think she's gone back to the library, she did say she was just trying to put off finishing her essay.' Would he have encouraged her if she had said a boy's name.

'Right, I see.'

A sort of damp pause. She could mention Grace. Sudden thought of her pale thin face. Perhaps best not to get his voice all over it. He must get mothers bringing their daughters to his surgery, he's a doctor after all, he must know more about it than she does. But even so – his close clever voice like that—

'Listen Annie' he says, sounding actually not very close, 'I've just got some pasta on, can I give you a ring back in about half an hour once I've eaten?'

'Oh' she says 'right.'

'Annie? Is that OK? Or twenty minutes even, it's nearly done.'

'Yes it's just—'

He can't go yet. She looks around the room at all her possessions stacked and shelved. Nothing offers a thought, they're all waiting for her – a sudden burst of Grace lying unconscious next door – and Miles and Katie – and her own stupid little world with her coffee and poems – she sees the two brown pieces on the shelf—

'I broke a mug' she says in the end.

'Ah.' He pauses, she can hear him wondering what on earth. 'What happened?'

'I don't know, I was washing it up, the handle just came off.'

'Are you OK, you didn't cut yourself or anything?'

'No no.'

'Oh good, and can you mend it do you think?'

'Yes – no, I mean, I can stick it back on but it won't be usable.'

'Yes I see.' His voice still not satisfied: he hasn't got to the bottom of this. 'Was it a special mug?' he says.

She nods, looking across the room at it. Its little brown form with no handle. The indignity of amputation.

'Annie?'

Oh, she is crying. Her chest and throat are all rising up. She tries to say 'I'm sorry I—'

'Annie?' he says. 'Are you OK?'

'Yes—'

Actually she isn't. She can't control it. This painful pinch. Something is wrong, all the way up to her throat it's too tight. She sucks in air, it *hurts*, she sobs—

'Annie what's wrong, has something happened?'

'No, I just—'

She just needs to get it under control. His warm voice is waiting for her on the other end. But it hurts, she can't do it, she just – she *wants* – she tries to inhale and half-sobs – she wants something dark and warm—

'Annie?'

—and the silent ambulance, flashing its lights and taking Grace away—

'Are you having a panic attack?' his voice says.

—she clutches at the previous thought – she wants to be, don't know, a small mouse in the pocket of the SCHOLAR's robes—

'I don't know' she whispers, 'maybe—'

—or a grasshopper in his pocket, or a glazed bead—

'*Annie*' he says with some force.

Everything hangs still.

'All right' he says, 'now listen to me, just sit down somewhere and we'll take some deep breaths, OK?'

'OK' she whispers. A glazed bead on a string. Or a glazed bead buried deep in the mud. She *wants*, he can't help her: she moans.

'All right,' she hears a saucepan being moved, 'are you sitting down?'

This one is a sob: '*Yes*.'

'Ohhkay, it's all right, we're just going to breathe in and out for a count of five, all right?'

She tries to fasten onto his voice. 'OK.'

'Right so now exhale all the way, and now *in*, two, three, four, five, and *out*, two, three, four, five, that's it, relax your stomach, and *in*, two, three,' and he keeps going. It suffocates her even more at first – she can't breathe, doesn't he understand? – but she tries not to gasp or gulp for air, and gradually it smooths out and she can do it. Tears are leaking onto her cheeks. He counts at least twenty cycles and she says nothing, just breathes.

When he finally says 'Better now?' she is damp and

drained through her insides. 'Yes' she says and sniffs some of the liquid back up.

'Good. Now have you had enough to eat and drink today?'

'Yes.'

'And are you sleeping properly?'

'Yes.'

'Good. Your doctor approves.'

She registers a placid little flicker of arousal.

'So has something happened or did it just come out of nowhere?'

'I miss you' she says.

Pause. She can hear him knowing this doesn't answer his question, deciding whether to stay in medical mode. Then his breath in: 'I miss you too. What's this about, hm?'

'I do want you to come and stay next weekend.'

'Oh no don't worry about that' he says, 'you don't have to decide now, we can talk tomorrow.'

'No, I do' she says. 'I've decided.'

'All right, if you're sure.'

'I am sure. I wish you were here now.'

She chose the right tone. He pauses. Then in a softer voice he says 'I'm just trying to work out how late I'd get to bed if I drove over now and stayed a couple of hours and drove home again.'

Oh it would destroy her energy and obliterate to-morrow's essay but – a fuck! tonight! in this very room! with his warm body! She whispers 'It's two hours' drive though.'

'Nah, less than that, especially going back, the roads would be empty' – then another exhale, 'ha well, I'd better not start thinking about it *too* much, I'd be a wreck for the

186

rest of the week. But OK, so do you want me to come Friday to Sunday so we get the whole weekend?'

He isn't coming tonight. 'Yes.'

'Right, and are you sure now? Sure sure?'

'Sure.'

'OK, I'll call the hotel. Here come the longest five days of my life.' He's smiling. His arms will be warm, maybe they'll wake up together in the dark morning and snuggle closer and wait for it to get light. 'Maybe we could get out of Oxford on the Sunday and go for a walk or something?'

'All right.' Her bundles of organs and nerves do not know what to make of this. They clump together in amazement, listening to her saying yes to his plans.

'Great, you go to Blackwell's in the week then and get a map or a book of walks and we can choose one. With a pub if you can. And then have a wander around the city on Saturday? By the way I'm so looking forward to everyone thinking I'm a married man and you're my bit on the side or something. Maybe I should bring you a little wedding ring to wear like if we were in the fifties.'

She laughs, a bit. Looks down at her bare left hand. Pictures it with a little gold wedding ring. 'You are joking' she says.

'More or less. We might get a few stares at breakfast I suppose. Although, I mean, there's not *that* much of an age difference really.'

The way Emma said Oooh boyfriend earlier. Like an alert going off. If anyone finds out his age it'll go round college like a swarm of bees. Maybe instead of going round all her places and bumping into all her people they could cut into Oxford at a new angle together: go to the art gallery and the canal, into Magdalen to see the deer park:

avoiding all the especial corners and lanes where she's had particular thoughts, the cafe she used to sit in with Miles. Flip Oxford over like a pillow and enjoy the new cold side—

'God I'm already thinking about your body.'

His voice has gone all dark. She takes a little breath in, a little sigh out, 'hm.'

'Maybe we should just stick the do not disturb sign on and stay in the room all weekend.'

She says shyly, softly 'What are you thinking about my body?'

'Oh god Annie don't go down that rabbit-hole, I need to have dinner and call the hotel.'

'You can tell me.' Why has she said it like that.

He takes a long breath in. 'Well. Since you ask. I er. I'm thinking about getting you on all fours and, and fucking you really slowly, really thoroughly.'

She lies back across the bed, holding the phone to her ear. Her left hand goes down to hold the metal button of her jeans between finger and thumb.

'And maybe' he continues, 'I mean, if you wanted, with your hands tied behind your back, maybe – ha.' He stops and takes a shaky breath.

She holds the thought. Her head pushed forward into the pillow – his hands on her hips pulling her back against him – the tightness through her shoulders with her arms back, and her wrists held stable behind her pelvis, and his whole body intent on fucking her – and what would he say, *that's* it, very gently—

'Annie?'

'Yeah I,' in as soft a voice as she can, 'I was just thinking about it.'

'Ha, all right, I have to stop now. You think about it a bit more and let me know when I see you.'

'OK' she says. She could do more than that. She could text him later: Maybe blindfolded? They could start something.

'But look are you all right now?' he says, 'do you want to talk about things any more, will you be all right?'

'Yeah but' – she searches, holding the little phone against her cheek – 'I wish you were here.'

'Well I will be soon thank god, I can't wait. I'll send you the details of the hotel once I've done the booking, OK?'

'Yes' she says softly.

He laughs: which is the correct interpretation. 'All right. Work very hard until then.'

'I will.' He really is stopping isn't he. It wouldn't be dignified to try and persuade him. 'See you soon.'

'Very soon, night night, sleep tight.'

'You too, bye.'

He is gone. She drops the phone and stretches out her arm into the duvet, rolling the stiff shoulder. The sloping ceiling stretches up away from her, like a rising question. He dealt with her very well, he was patient and soothing. Trying to keep up with her sudden swings of temperature. And he stopped being her doctor as soon as she was all right again.

She sits on the edge of the bed. And so he will come next weekend. The whole room heard her say she wants him to come. Steady, then. Steady thy laden head across a brook. And maybe things will find a new realm. When he said, with your hands behind your back, her mind did some kind of new manoeuvre and got hold of something. It wasn't precisely what he said. Just adjacent to it. More like, if he could murmur, This will be very good for you, or There now, that's better isn't it, and tightening his grip he fucks her. The whole tone of it, the whole premise. She could write on a piece of paper I WANT in big letters. She needs – something—

A thought flickers out again and catches the light, she sees it clearly, the big obscure thing that she wants, and then it vanishes off into her mind's forest.

She decides: she won't call home tonight, she can speak to them all tomorrow. Enough words for one day. Time to be very, very quiet.

Calmly, like a nun undressing in front of her wooden cross, she takes off each piece of her clothing and puts it on her chair or in her washing bag. She goes into the bathroom, turns the shower on and sticks her hand in, testing the water until it comes hot. Then gets in and pulls the door closed. The hot water pours down through her head and shoulders and back, her body shrinks and shivers, then it remembers what warmth is and all her nerve cells tilt upwards to meet it. Ohhh this gorgeous heat. The glass door already fogged, steam is building in the cubicle: she is alone in this white world. Lifts her arms: her puffs of caramel hair wilt under the water.

She and Rich do have, she doesn't know what it is, but something good, something warm like this, pouring them together. She squeezes shampoo into her hand and makes a cap of lather over her hair, getting her fingertips deeply all over her scalp, then puts her head back under the *real heat*, god yes, and lets the rinse run all down through her hair and over her shoulders. It is something muscular they have, as if he is now securely in her tissue fibres, her body knows to long for his body.

Soon they will have to tell. If they are to see each other at Easter and in the summer, they will have to tell. At home, as she pulls conditioner through her heavy wet hair, at home she is the most private of all of them, it is well known, but she is not all-out secretive. Over Christmas the speaking of actual lies about where she was going was unpleasant and tedious, and slightly frightening. Mum wouldn't shout, she never shouts, but nor has she ever tried to thwart any of her daughters, or been thwarted by them in turn. She has the sharpest haircut and the longest neck and the straightest back, and goes about to lectures and dinners intensely discussing university politics, the symphonies of Mahler, the changing ideologies of Russian communism, but she is so tender with her daughters, she greets them coming down the stairs with a stroke of her hand over their heads. Yes, she will have to be told.

She rinses the slippery chemicals out of her hair. Maybe when orchestra season ends and Mum won't see him every week. Then if it's really bad he can leave the orchestra. Soaps herself all across the planes of her body and into all the creases, lathers up the three patches of hair, twists about rinsing herself under the water, peels her buttocks apart briefly to let the water in, tips her head back to send one last soak of heat down through her head. He said it cheerfully: I don't mind taking a break from it, all the rehearsals have felt a bit much lately anyway. Or I can find a different orchestra, there must be another one that needs a substandard violinist.

She turns the shower off. Sudden dripping quiet. She divides her hair into two wet ropes and squeezes the water out of each, shakes water off her legs and arms, and pushes open the shower door: emerges damp and triumphant into the bathroom. The clean Sunday evening towel, folded and slightly stiff: she shakes it out, and dries herself in sections. An image of the SCHOLAR, standing naked after his bath, flipping his head forward and scrubbing at his wet hair with a towel, then combing it back rapidly, getting ready to go down to dinner. She smiles as she draws the thick clean pyjamas up over her warm legs. Off he goes fretting.

~

With her hair blown hot and dry and secured into a smooth night-time plait, she fills the kettle again and sets it to boil. Turns her back on it as the noise fills the room, and goes to brush her teeth. In the bathroom she makes herself stand in front of the mirror and watches herself put the toothbrush in her mouth: *these* her brown eyes, looking at *those* her brown eyes, with vigorous white and blue movement just below. So this is her face. She lowers her face to spit in the sink and comes up all foamy-mouthed. Wipes her mouth with a wet hand. Then goes back into the bedroom and over to her shelves, picks up the packet of camomile and fills the little mesh infuser with dried flowers, puts it into her pink and white striped mug, and pours hot water in. Does the calming power come from the camomile itself, or simply from the intention to be calm. For a second she looks at the two pieces of broken brown mug and something furious starts to rise up – both how much she cares and how stupid it is to care – so she takes her tea and turns away. Sits down: and decides to make herself think, for at least a few minutes she will think, about Grace.

Deep breath, and so. Grace on a drip in a white hospital, her thin blonde hair, her exhausted face. Her parents on the road up from Exeter, driving in distraught silence. Anorexia: a horror-word. A clever, nimble vacuum, a colourless force like wind, sneaking flesh off the bones every day in tiny morsels. The wish to eat well becomes something like No I must not eat, or Although I know I must eat I don't want to, or My body will no longer accept food and I am helpless against it – or do all these modalities become indistinct. Or is there a sharp light of ecstasy, does Grace *enjoy* – does it magnify her sense of the ancients, do Ovid and Homer and Aeschylus blaze skeletally brighter—

No, she tells herself in her world-voice. No. She is ill.

Next door is Grace's room fiendishly neat, or left in disarray. Was she creeping around getting weaker and weaker. It must be so relentless: she must be so tired. At what point did the illness confine her inside. If – a small rush of thought – if at lunchtime seeing Grace's food in the fridge – what was the expiry date on the soups – if it had occurred to her to also think, actually when *did* I last see Grace, if she had gone and knocked on her door. Would she getting no answer have shrugged and come back to her sonnets. Could she have pinned a note to the door, or sent her a text or email, or – but so could any of the classicists, so could many people who would have noticed Grace not showing up to things.

She takes a hot sip of camomile. Closes her eyes for a moment and tries to accept her portion of blame. Or responsibility, if that is different. She could see if Grace would like her to visit. Ring the hospital in the next couple of days, perhaps, and as soon as Grace is well enough get a bus up the hill to see her. This is not what the SCHOLAR would do: but very clearly this is what she should do.

A mage is asked a difficult question: he sits down under a tree: he fasts until he finds an answer. A perfectly natural way of waiting for knowledge. A pause in the system. Why then in Oxford is knowledge thought to require weighing down with feasts and good wine, and tea and scones, and long speeches. And they never (her mind turns off onto a forking path) they never ask really good, really specific, really difficult and interesting questions. If only there was someone who could ask her those questions. A spiritual director. A teacher, in the fullest sense of the word: someone whose attention is skilful and snug. A personal, *personal* tutor.

A hazardous line of thought: and also, exquisitely soothing.

She thinks of the black pond. She thinks of priests. She thinks of a priest moving the heavy folds of his vestments aside to release his cock. And she thinks – this is not what she originally meant, but – she thinks of attending to him on her knees, accepting his mastery, while he grasps the carved arms of his chair. No. This is not what she meant. She tries again: a priest who sits behind a desk and takes her seriously and gives mild thoughtful responses to each of her dilemmas.

Anyway. She puts her hand into her pyjama top, against her breastbone – feels the this-ness, the here-ness of it: the place where she resides. Then she goes and picks up her phone from the bed and sends in quick succession five messages: one to Sophy, one to Mum, one to Bridget, one to Ciara, and one to Rich. As she presses Send on the last one she wishes for an oaten biscuit she could nibble on. An unusual thought. As if she has offered out five biscuits, and can now take one for herself. And really *taste* the grains separating and disintegrating between her teeth. The final message has sent: with evening finality she turns the phone off, and puts it back on the shelf.

Night has fallen. She thinks it quite deliberately, in one phrase, drinking her warm good camomile. She has reached the end of the day. All the voices pouring up and down phone lines and busying together in the dining hall – these many, many people, each one a vast, an immense person with attributes and ambitions and unsuspected privacies – all over for another day.

She sips. Camomile is a soft clean cotton drink. There ought to be something strong and dark for getting into the subterranean depths of an evening: whisky perhaps, or cognac: for sitting going patiently through a long melancholy book. Lamp, armchair. Not even pretending night hasn't fallen. Small gusts of longing are allowed to come through every twenty, thirty pages. She recognises it as the SCHOLAR: who will always try to find one more thing, just one more, before giving up and going to bed.

She smiles suddenly. Today has been – She gets up in a quick movement and goes to the dark window, her body still glowing warm from the shower. She raises the back of her hand to her mouth and crushes her lips solidly, affectionately, against her own wristbone. Out there somewhere are the SCHOLAR and SEDUCER, this is where she will settle them, reconciled in the dark street, heading off together for a drink.

Then in an unforeseen move she goes to her desk, clicks the lamp on, sits down in her dressing gown and bare feet, and pulls towards her a piece of paper. Takes a pen and writes:

In a world where sonnets exist, only sonnets need exist.

197

Looks at it. Replies to herself 'I have no idea.' Studies the paper for another moment. Then turns the desk lamp off and leaves the thought there: for consideration tomorrow.

She goes back to the window: twists the catch and pushes it wide open. The cold air touches her face and hands and neck. She looks into the darkness, the far-off wash of sound from the city. She can feel, somewhere in her head, wispy thoughts clumping and separating, like thin clouds racing across the moon. Watching the darkness steadily she feels the shivers start to come on, knowing they will not harm her. She feels the integrity of her strong body like an apricot, and the system of weights and measures where her mind moves around making night-time conversions.

A black and gold patterned joy spreads through her. She pulls the window shut: this is fine. This is very fine.

THE END

ACKNOWLEDGEMENTS

For the writing of this book I am indebted most of all to Shakespeare's astonishing sonnets: their directness, their agility, and their extraordinary emotional nuance. Virginia Woolf in her diary (13 April 1930) perhaps expresses best the writer's helplessness in the face of Shakespeare: 'Evidently the pliancy of his mind was so complete that he could furbish out any train of thought; &, relaxing lets fall a shower of such unregarded flowers. Why then should anyone else attempt to write. This is not "writing" at all.'

I also took inspiration from criticism on Shakespeare by R. P. Blackmur, William Empson, and Ernest Sutherland Bates, and from Helen Vendler's wonderful commentary *The Art of Shakespeare's Sonnets*.

It's also a pleasure to express thanks for the support and encouragement I was given while writing and editing this book. Thank you to Tiffany Atkinson, Laura Joyce, Clare Connors, Philip Langeskov, Karen Schaller, and Nonia Williams. Thank you to the Arts and Humanities Faculty at the University of East Anglia for awarding me the PhD studentship during which the novel was written. Thank you to Jon McGregor.

Thank you to my agent Tracy Bohan, and all at the Wylie Agency. Thank you to my editors Lettice Franklin and

Mitzi Angel, and all at Weidenfeld & Nicolson and Farrar, Straus and Giroux. Thank you to Emily Stokes, Lidija Haas, and Amanda Gersten, and all at the *Paris Review*, in which an excerpt of the novel appeared.

Thank you to early readers of the novel: Al Bell, Anna Bryant, Pip Carter, Olivia Heal, Kasia Stringer-Ladds, and Georgia Walker Churchman. Thank you to many more teachers, friends and fellows; thank you to Linda Street and Nando Messias; and thank you to my beloved, Doug Evans.

Thank you above all to my family, particularly Nicky Brown, Tony Brown, and Lorna Williamson.